Dear Re

Welcome to So
property in the Star Valley and home to Reid, Kane
and Annie McKinnon.

There really is a beautiful and remote Star Valley
and it's situated to the north of Townsville where I
live. The Broken and Star Rivers flow through this
district and the cattle stations there have wonderful
names like Starlight, Starbright and ZigZag.
However, there are no towns in the valley and
although I have made Southern Cross Station and
the township of Mirrabrook as authentic as I can,
they are entirely my creations.

I am thrilled to be bringing you three linked stories
about the McKinnon family's secrets. In this book,
Kane's secret is the first to be exposed, when
Charity Denham arrives from England searching
for her missing brother.

Little does Kane know that once Charity comes
into his life, his heart is also at risk….

Happy reading and my warmest wishes,

Barbara Hannay.

Southern Cross Ranch

Family secrets, Outback marriages!

**Deep in the heart of the Outback,
nestled in Star Valley, is the McKinnon family
cattle station. Southern Cross Station is an
oasis in the harsh Outback landscape and a
refuge to the McKinnon family—Kane, Reid and
their sister Annie. But it's also full of secrets...**

This month is Kane's story. He's keeping a secret,
but little does he know that by helping a
friend he'll also find a bride!
The Cattleman's English Rose

Then it's Annie's turn. How's a young woman
supposed to find love when the nearest eligible
man lives miles away? Easy, she arranges a blind
date on the Internet! But her date has a secret...
The Blind Date Surprise (on sale in April)

And lastly, Reid. He's about to discover
a secret that will change his whole life!
Luckily his childhood sweetheart is determined
to help him to discover the mysteries of his past—
and help him find love along the way!
The Mirrabrook Marriage (on sale in May)

THE CATTLEMAN'S
ENGLISH ROSE

Barbara Hannay

> *Southern Cross Ranch*

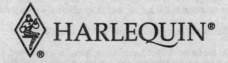

TORONTO • NEW YORK • LONDON
AMSTERDAM • PARIS • SYDNEY • HAMBURG
STOCKHOLM • ATHENS • TOKYO • MILAN • MADRID
PRAGUE • WARSAW • BUDAPEST • AUCKLAND

For Elliot, who inspired me
with his stories about the real Star Valley.

ISBN 0-373-18187-6

THE CATTLEMAN'S ENGLISH ROSE

First North American Publication 2005.

www.eHarlequin.com

Printed in U.S.A.

CHAPTER ONE

'WHO'S that?'

The woman on the stool beside Kane McKinnon gave his thigh an impatient squeeze as she squinted towards the bar-room doorway.

'Who's what?' Kane refused to look and took a lazy sip of his beer instead.

'That girl, of course.' She tugged at Kane's jeans and he knew she wanted him to turn and join her in a scrutiny of someone who'd just come into the Mirrabrook pub. Perversely, he let his gaze linger on his glass.

There was nothing on earth quite so important as the first icy-cold drink on a stinking hot day, especially when a man had been out in the bush on a cattle muster for three weeks. Besides, Marsha's possessive touch was bugging him.

Admittedly, he'd been in a bad mood all day, thanks to the shocker of a bombshell his little sister had dropped that morning.

He and his brother, Reid, had arrived back

at Southern Cross homestead just after dawn, ready for breakfast, their stomachs primed for a good feed of steak and eggs, and they'd been greeted by a cold, empty stove and a note propped against the sugar bowl in the middle of the kitchen table.

They'd read their little sister's note twice before it had sunk in that Annie had taken off to the city for a week—maybe two...*for a date with destiny,* she had written. *But don't worry about me, I'll be quite safe. I'll be staying with Melissa Browne.*

It was totally out of character for Annie to up and leave them without warning. Not that the kid didn't deserve a trip to the city now and then, but she knew that her brothers would need time to find a replacement housekeeper while she was away.

As it was, Kane had been forced to waste a good few hours driving into Mirrabrook today to track down someone to help them out at short notice. And, damn it, there was no one available.

At least, there were no 'safe women' available—sensible women, who wouldn't view a chance to work at Southern Cross for the McKinnon brothers as an open invitation to start dreaming about a long white dress and a trip to the altar.

'I've never seen her before, have you?' Marsha was still talking about the woman who'd just walked in and her voice sounded as disgruntled as Kane felt.

He shrugged. Marsha regarded every woman as competition, which perhaps explained why her shorts kept getting shorter and her necklines lower. The top she was wearing today wasn't much bigger than a Band-Aid.

It was another thing that added to his irritation. He didn't like women to be prudes, but Marsha's recent taste in clothes and her increasingly possessive body language smacked of desperation. And that was a definite turn-off.

'Why is she staring at you?' Marsha hissed.

'I have no idea.' Kane sighed, hoping she would catch his not so subtle hint that he found her question tedious.

'Well, you're about to find out.'

Slipping from her stool, Marsha moved close, so close that her bosom bumped against Kane and he turned to see why she was making such a fuss.

Struth.

Every sunburned, jeans-clad local in the Mirrabrook pub was gaping at the newcomer.

And Kane saw why.

To start with, she was wearing a dress—a soft, summery, knee-length number, the colour of ripe limes. And her skin was milk-white, her hair long and wavy, the colour of expensive brandy.

Against a backdrop of empty beer glasses, bar-stools and outback ringers draped over a pool table, the young woman looked as if she'd walked off the set of an elegant, old-fashioned romantic movie and found herself in the wrong scene.

But the most surprising thing about her was that she was heading straight for him, her smoky green eyes resolute and unflinching, and Kane thought of Joan of Arc facing up to the Brits. A woman on a mission.

He felt an urgent need to slide off the bar-stool and stand tall. His right hand was damp from the condensation on his beer glass and he gave it a surreptitious wipe on the back of his jeans.

'Kane McKinnon?' the girl said when she reached him. With only a slight nod of acknowledgement towards Marsha, she held out her slim white hand. 'I'm Charity Denham. I believe you know my brother, Tim.'

Tim Denham's sister. This was a surprise. Her green eyes were watching him carefully, but Kane made sure his gaze didn't falter. She didn't look much like her brother, although they both had the same well-bred English accents.

'Tim Denham?' he said. 'Sure, I know him.'

They exchanged cautious handshakes.

'I understand that Tim worked for you on Southern Cross station,' she said.

'That's right. He was on one of our mustering teams. Are you out here on a holiday?'

'No.'

She dropped her gaze and pressed her lips together, as if she were gathering strength for what she had to say next and he decided that her bravado had been a front. Then she looked up at him again.

Her eyes were the dusky green of young gum leaves and her skin so fine and pale he could almost see through it.

'I'm looking for my brother,' she said.

'Any special reason?'

She seemed startled by his question, as if the answer was as obvious as Marsha's cleavage. 'Tim's missing. My father and I haven't heard from him in over a month.'

Beside him, Marsha let out an impatient snort. 'A month? That's nothing. Tim Denham's old enough to look after himself.

He doesn't need his sister chasing halfway across the world to look out for him.'

'Let me introduce Marsha,' Kane cut in.

The two women exchanged cool, cut-glass smiles.

'Can we get you a drink?' he asked.

'A lemon lime and bitters would be nice, thank you.'

'I'll get it,' offered Marsha.

Her eagerness surprised Kane, but he pushed some notes towards her from the pile of change on the table. 'Thanks, Marsh.'

As he drained his glass, Marsha said to Charity, 'You don't want that drink. I'll get you a gin and tonic. That's what you English girls drink, isn't it?'

'Oh.' There was a momentary hesitation. 'Well, just a small one then, thank you.'

Marsha sashayed off to the other end of the bar and the English girl watched her thoughtfully.

'Pull up a pew,' Kane said, nodding towards a bar-stool.

She sat on it gingerly and kept her neat white hands folded demurely in her lap, while he resumed his usual position, with the heel of one riding boot hooked over the rung of the stool and the other leg stretched out comfortably.

'How did you track me down?' he asked.

'I asked for directions to Southern Cross at the post office. The woman there told me you were in town today and that I'd find you here.'

That would be right. It wasn't possible to blow your nose in this town without Rhonda at the post office knowing about it and passing the news on to everyone else.

'Mr McKinnon.' The determination in the girl's voice suggested that she planned to interview him rather than conduct a pleasant conversation. 'I'm hoping that you can help me to find my brother.'

'You shouldn't worry about him. He can look after himself.'

'But we haven't heard anything in over a month and Tim knew how much Father and I would worry. Father made him swear on the Bible that he'd keep us posted about his whereabouts.'

'On the Bible?' Kane had difficulty in hiding his surprise.

'Didn't Tim tell you that our father is the rector of St Alban's, Hollydean?'

'Ah—no.'

'Father only agreed to pay Tim's airfare to Australia on the condition that he stayed in touch. And up until a month ago we received regular updates, but since then there's been total silence.'

'You mustn't worry. He's okay.'

Excitement sparked in her eyes. 'Do you know that for sure? Do you know where he is?'

He winced. 'What I meant was Tim's an okay bloke. He can look after himself.'

'But he knows so little about Australia.'

'You underestimate your brother. When he worked for me he picked things up quickly and he fitted in well. Of course, he copped a bit of a ribbing from some of the boys about his toff accent, but he's a good worker. He was good with horses.'

'But where did he go from here? When did he leave?'

'He took off about four or five weeks ago, but I can't tell you where.'

'Can't or won't?'

Her quick question almost caught him off guard. *Almost.* 'I can't tell you,' he said in a take-it-or-leave-it tone. 'All I know is he's left the district.'

She frowned. 'It just doesn't seem right. Didn't Tim tell you anything about where he was going, or what he was going to do?'

Kane shrugged. 'This is a free country.'

She shook her head and dragged in a deep, dissatisfied breath through her nose.

'Out here, people can come and go as they please,' Kane said in defence. 'It happens all the time. Isn't that what travelling is all about? Being free to take up whatever opportunities arise?' He shot her a deliberate, searching glance. 'Maybe your brother wants to cut the apron strings.'

Her response was to glare at him, but he merely smiled.

'You can't keep a young bloke like Tim on a short chain for ever.'

She gave an impatient toss of her bright brandy hair. 'That's more or less what the police said, but I won't accept that.'

'So you've already been to the police?'

'Of course. I spoke to them in Townsville. They've listed Tim as missing, but they were far too casual for my liking. They spun me the line that young people go missing all the time. They said that most of the youngsters are deliberately running away, but I *know* that Tim wouldn't do that.'

'How can you be so sure?'

There was a warning flash of green fire in her eyes. 'I know my brother. I've raised him since our mother died when he was seven years old.'

This time Kane couldn't hide his surprise. 'You must have been very young to take on that kind of responsibility.'

'I was fourteen.'

'You've done a grand job.' He switched his gaze from her earnest face to the bottom of his beer glass. 'So what else did the police tell you?'

She sighed. 'Not much. They've checked Tim's bank account and there haven't been any withdrawals. They say that's good, because his account hasn't been stripped and that suggests that there hasn't been foul play. But if Tim hasn't used his money, couldn't it mean that he's had an accident? He might have perished somewhere and no one knows about it.'

'I wouldn't start panicking just yet,' Kane said gently. 'I paid him in cash, so he would have been well stocked up when he left here.'

The *clip-clip* of Marsha's heels sounded on the wooden floor. As she reached their table and handed out glasses, she eyed them both with a sweet-and-sour smile. They thanked her and took their time sampling grateful sips of their cold drinks.

The silence was broken by the clink of ice against glass and then another sigh from Charity. 'I know I must look like a fussy mother hen, but I can't help worrying,' she said. 'Tim's so young. He's only just turned nineteen.'

There was a short gasp of surprise from Marsha. Kane shot her a sharp, silencing frown.

'Out here, if a boy's nineteen, he's old enough to vote, old enough to drink and old enough to fight and die for his country,' he said.

'That may be so, but I intend to find him. If you can't help me, could you suggest where I should start looking?'

He shrugged. 'He could be anywhere.'

Her eyes narrowed. 'I'm sure you can do better than that.'

Kane sighed. He should have known from the moment she walked in that this girl was a crusader who wouldn't give in easily.

'Okay, I'll give it to you straight.' With a forefinger, he ticked off the fingers on his left hand. 'Your brother could have taken another mustering job on a property farther out, or he could be droving cattle up north in the Cape, which would mean spending six or eight weeks on horseback. He could be fishing for barramundi up in the Gulf, or he could be on a prawn trawler out of Karumba.' He eyed her slowly. 'You want some more?'

When she didn't answer, he gave a slight shake of his head before continuing. 'He might be gold prospecting out the back of Croydon, or fossicking for sapphires down at Annakie, or he could be sitting on a bar-stool chatting up a Swedish backpacker on Magnetic Island.'

As she listened to his list she chewed her lower lip—her soft, petal-pink lip—and he couldn't help staring.

She shook her head. 'But if Tim was doing any of those things he could have phoned us, emailed or written a letter.'

Kane shrugged again. 'I'd say he's too busy, or too remote.'

Charity stared into her glass, swilled the ice cubes and took another thoughtful sip of her drink.

'Trust me,' Kane said quietly, keeping the expression on his face deadpan. 'Your brother's okay.'

'But how do you know that?'

Abruptly he drained his second beer. 'Look, you don't want to hang around here. This isn't the place for you. You should head back to the coast. Why don't you see a bit of Australia? Have a bit of a holiday while you're out here. I have Tim's home address. I'll contact you if I hear something.'

He knew she wouldn't be happy to be dismissed so soon, but she'd asked her questions, he had answered them and now he wanted her to leave.

To his surprise she accepted this.

With a series of nervous gulps she finished her gin and tonic. 'Thanks for the drink,' she said. 'I was hoping you could help me, Mr McKinnon, but as you can't I'll try to find someone else in this district who might have known Tim.'

Then she jumped to her feet and was just a little unsteady. How much gin had Marsha put in that drink?

Holding out her hand, she said, 'Thanks for your time.'

'Just remember my advice,' he said. Her hand felt soft and he was conscious of her delicate bones as he clasped it. 'Don't hang around here. Get back to the coast and have some fun.'

She turned to Marsha, who looked decidedly chipper all of a sudden. 'It was nice to meet you, Marsha.'

'You, too, Charity,' she said, giving a little wave.

Holding her head high, Charity turned and walked very carefully across the bare wooden floor to the bar's entrance. Kane remembered

the conviction in her eyes when she'd entered
the bar not so long ago, and he wasn't proud
that he'd managed to knock the stuffing out
of her so easily.

Thanks for nothing, Mr McKinnon.

As soon as Charity reached the little foyer
at the front of the pub, she slumped on to a
wooden bench, swamped by anger and disappointment.

She'd come all this way and she'd pinned
so much hope on Kane McKinnon's help and
all he would tell her was to get out of the
district.

There'd been an air of secrecy about him
that disturbed her. Was it a natural reticence
or a wall of defence because he had something
to hide? She couldn't shake off the feeling that
he'd been warning her off or, worse still, that
his words had been a threat.

But if he wouldn't help, where else could
she go for assistance? The police had been
next to no help and she had no one else to
turn to. She was in a strange country as vast
and alien as the moon and she couldn't think
what to do next.

Kane McKinnon had suggested that Tim
was having such a wonderful time that he'd
simply forgotten to keep in touch. Could that

be true? Had she been expecting too much of her brother? Perhaps the boy had fallen head over heels in love. It was possible, but it didn't really explain his silence.

'Your Tim was a cutie.'

Startled, Charity turned to see Marsha. 'Oh, hello.'

'He was a real gentleman,' Marsha said, stepping closer. The huge silver loops in her ears made soft *tink-tink* sounds when she moved.

'Did you know Tim very well?'

'Well enough.' The woman's face was a picture of sympathy as she plonked down on the seat next to Charity. 'To be honest, I thought Kane was a bit rough on you. After all, you've come such a long way and you don't know anyone here.'

Charity's eyes widened, signalling her deepening surprise.

'Why don't you come with me? We can have a nice little chat about your problem. Girl to girl.'

'That's kind of you,' said Charity, trying to hide her surprise.

Marsha was very different from the kind of women who normally befriended her and the last person she'd expected to offer the hand of friendship was Kane's woman. At least, she assumed Marsha was Kane McKinnon's girl-friend. No doubt he had a string of girlfriends. She supposed that most women would find his silver-blue eyes and hard packed, lean body attractive.

Marsha smiled. 'Why don't we go and have a quiet drink in the beer garden?'

'Oh, thank you…'

How could she refuse? She had so few options it would be foolish to do so. Charity rose and followed the other woman through a side door into a surprisingly pretty, shaded court-yard. The area was paved with black and white tiles and protected from the sun by a vine-covered pergola. A border of huge fern-filled hanging baskets made the area feel very secluded.

'It's quieter out here,' Marsha said, nodding towards the only other couple, who were seated at a far table.

'It's lovely.'

'You take a seat while I get us another drink.'

'Please, let me pay.' Charity pulled her purse from her handbag, but Marsha dismissed her with a wave of her hand. 'You can get the next round,' she said with a grin.

Charity doubted that she could handle a third round. Perhaps it was the heat, but the

first drink had left her feeling just a little unsteady but, before she could say so, Marsha
disappeared.

She returned very quickly. 'Cheers,' she
said, clinking her glass against Charity's.

'Cheers.' Charity took a small sip. 'Do you
work in Mirrabrook?'

'Sure do. I have my own hairdressing salon.
I've stacks of clients. Most days I'm run off
my feet.'

'You must be good.' After another sip, she
set her glass down. 'Was there something you
wanted to tell me about Tim?'

The silver earrings tinkled as Marsha leaned
closer and lowered her voice. 'Just between
you, me and the gate post, I'm a bit worried
about the dear boy. Tim promised to see me
on my birthday, but he didn't turn up.'

'He promised to see *you?*' Shocked,
Charity picked up her glass and drank deeply.

Marsha smiled slowly. 'Does that surprise
you?'

'I—er—it does a bit.' She didn't want to
think why Tim would visit Marsha. She
couldn't even begin to let her mind go there.

'It didn't make sense that he disappeared,'
Marsha said.

'So you think something's happened
to him?'

Marsha frowned. 'I'm not sure, but I'm happy to help you find out.'

'That's so kind.' Charity wondered if she'd misjudged this woman. Perhaps she'd been leaping to all the wrong conclusions.

Marsha smiled again and reached out and squeezed Charity's hand. 'Drink up. I'm sure we women can work something out.'

CHAPTER TWO

CHARITY looked for Tim everywhere.

Racing through the rectory on winged feet, she searched every room, under every bed and inside every cupboard. She flew up to the attic, then charged back down to the kitchen to check the pantry. As a last resort she checked the study, although she was quite sure her little brother would never venture uninvited into the hallowed sanctum where their father wrote his sermons.

Tim wasn't there.

Outside, a storm raged—a noisy, boisterous storm that rattled the window frames and sent tree branches thudding on the roof.

Dashing to the window, she peered frantically into the black night and saw the stained glass windows of St Alban's church glowing like gemstones through the dark, driving rain.

Grabbing a raincoat, she ran out into the storm. She tried to call Tim, but the wind and the rain whipped the words away and she *hadn't thought to bring a torch, so she had to feel her way forward like a blind person.*

'Tim, please, where are you? I can't bear this awful worry.'

Then, somehow, she knew the answer to her own question. He was in the graveyard.

A bolt of lightning lit up the churchyard, showing her the way through the dark night. On legs rubbery with fear, she scurried past the yew tree behind the church, ducking between the gravestones, slipping on the wet grass and trying not to think of ghosts.

She found Tim huddled on the grave where their dear mother lay.

Such a forlorn, shivering, little boy of seven, clinging to a block of cold marble, his black hair plastered to his head and his pyjamas soaked through.

Her heart broke as she swept him into her arms. He clung to her and he was as wet and slippery as a frog, with bony elbows and knees.

'I want Mummy,' he sobbed. 'I want her. I want her to come back.'

'Oh, darling.'

She couldn't be angry with him. All she could do was cuddle him close and cover him with kisses. 'I'm here, sweetheart. I love you. You must let me be mummy now.'

To her horror the boy struggled out of her arms and took off, running away from her into the stormy night.

'You're no good. You keep losing me,' he cried.

And he disappeared into the black.

'Tim! No! Please don't go. Come back!'

Charity's terrified cry woke her.

She tried to open her eyes. *Ouch!* Blinding stripes of sunlight blasted through the Venetian blinds and she snapped her eyes shut again as the trauma of her dream was replaced by reality.

Tim *was* missing. In Australia.

And then she was aware of physical pain. Her head. And *yuck!* Her mouth tasted like the bottom of a bird's cage.

What had happened?

All she could remember of the previous night was having a long, cosy chat with Marsha. Actually…it had been rather a one-sided chat. She had listened while the other woman talked. Marsha had told her about Tim…about what a lovely fellow he was… And Charity had a vague memory that Marsha had insisted they keep drinking if she wanted to hear everything about her brother.

But if she'd learned anything significant it was lost to her now. At some point the conversation had shifted to Kane and his brother, Reid…but she couldn't remember anything much. Except Marsha's clear warning to stay away from Kane…

She felt vile. Awful. This had to be a hangover. Her first. And where on earth was she?

Keeping her eyes closed, she lay very still while she explored her surroundings with her hands. There was a mattress, a pillow beneath her head and a sheet covering her. Carefully she turned her head away from the bright window, opened one eye and squinted and discovered that the light on this side of the room was more hangover-friendly.

Okay. There was no doubt that she was in a bedroom. But where was this room?

Bravely, she opened the other eye and took in details. The room was simply furnished, its only decoration a dried arrangement of Australian wildflowers on an old-fashioned pine dresser. The walls were a dingy off-white and an ugly mustard and brown striped rug covered most of the floor. A doorway led to an adjoining room.

It had to be a bathroom, because she could hear the sound of running water. And splashes.

Splashes? *Good grief.* Splashes meant someone was in the bathroom. It meant…

Before she could come to terms with what it meant, the running water stopped.

For five seconds there was silence except for the desperate thumping of her heartbeats in her ears. And then footsteps.

And a tall figure appeared in the doorway.

Kane McKinnon.

She felt deprived of oxygen. How on earth had she ended up in a bedroom with *him*?

He was wearing nothing but blue jeans and, although she didn't want to, she couldn't help staring at him—at his bronzed skin, which looked as if it had been polished to a high sheen—at his broad shoulders, his taut torso, and his muscles—his *exceptional* muscles.

Kane and his muscles strolled into her room and he stood at the end of her bed, looking down at her.

She tried to ask him what he was doing in her room—what *she* was doing there—but when she opened her mouth no words came.

'Good morning,' he drawled.

So it *was* morning.

Which meant…there'd been a *night*. But where and when and…*how*?

'Good—' Charity gulped. 'Morning.' If only her mouth wasn't so parched. 'W-where are we?'

A ghost of a smile played at the corners of

his mouth. 'We're in a cabin at the back of the Mirrabrook pub. Don't you remember?'

'No.' Pain pounded behind her eyes and she closed them, but she felt too vulnerable with her eyes closed while Kane towered at the foot of her bed, so she squinted at him. 'What are you doing in my bedroom?'

'I beg your pardon, Miss Denham, but you should rephrase that question.'

'Why?' she asked faintly, dreading the answer.

'This is *my* room.'

Her eyes flashed wide again. 'Then how—?' She had to stop and wet her lips with her tongue. 'Why am I—' *Oh, help.* 'How did I get here?'

'I carried you.'

Lord have mercy.

A mocking smile tweaked his lips. 'I found you in the beer garden with Marsha, tossing back drinks like a ringer. Marsha's used to grog, but you were on the verge of passing out and in need of a bed, and—' He shrugged his massive bare shoulders. 'This was the only room left.'

'I see. I suppose I should thank you.'

He walked the length of the bed to her side and her breath caught. It was unnerving to have Kane McKinnon so undressed...and so close to her bed. What was he doing here? What had happened last night?

She shivered at the thought that this mega-masculine body might have lain next to her, that she might have…they might have…

Had she touched that satiny skin?

No. Surely not.

She realised he'd brought her a glass of water and two pain-killers.

'I imagine you'll need these.'

'Thanks,' she said, but she didn't take them. There were too many important questions that had to be clarified. 'You didn't sleep here—with—with me, did you?'

His eyes were the silvery-blue of an early morning sky and now they glinted with suppressed amusement. 'I didn't have any choice. I told you this was the only cabin left.'

'But why couldn't you have gone home? Why did you stay here?'

'I had to make sure you were okay.'

Was that true? Was she supposed to be grateful? What kind of man was Kane McKinnon? She had no idea whether he was trustworthy. The tanned skin on his face was cut by a pale scar that sliced through his right eyebrow and almost reached his eyelid and she couldn't help wondering what had caused it.

'What did we—? We didn't— Did we— um—' How on earth did she ask this? 'We didn't—make love or—or anything, did we?'

She saw a flash of white teeth as he grinned. 'Make love? Hell, no.'

'Thank heavens,' she whispered and felt some of her tension let go.

'I don't think I'd call it love,' he said in a slow drawl.

Charity braced herself for the worst. The tension returned one hundred fold.

'What we had was more like straight out lust—'

'No!'

'Simple, uncomplicated sex,' he said and the blue eyes gleamed.

A horrified moan escaped her. Wrenching the sheet over her, she cowered beneath it. But now, with her eyes closed, she saw a vision of all the devout women in her father's parish staring at their rector's reprobate, drunken daughter with scandalised, open-mouthed horror.

Kane's voice reached her through her shame. 'Don't worry, sweet Charity. It was wild.'

'Go away!'

'You were fabulous—sensational.'

Her head shot above the sheet. 'Stop it! You're despicable.' She hated him.

But she was also beginning to suspect that he was lying. Surely he was teasing her?

Emboldened by the thought, she lowered her gaze...and saw...

...that she was fully dressed.

Every bit of clothing was still in its proper place, except for her shoes. *Thank heavens.*

She spun sideways to check the other side of the room and winced because the movement made her head hurt. There was another bed beneath the window, a twin of hers, and its rumpled sheets indicated that Kane had slept there.

He'd definitely been teasing her...which made him even more despicable, because she was left feeling foolish for leaping to assumptions.

'If that's Australian humour, I don't think much of it,' she snapped.

'Come on, take these,' he said again, pressing the tablets into her hand.

She had little choice but to sit up and accept the tablets and glass of water and to swallow obediently, but she wouldn't look at him. She didn't want to see that mocking amusement in his eyes.

He said, 'I've brought your bags up, so be

a good girl and hop into the shower. Then you need a big recovery breakfast before you leave.'

'But I don't plan to leave.' She couldn't let this embarrassing situation throw her. No doubt Kane McKinnon was still trying to scare her away, but she had to remember her mission—why she was here. Tim was still out there in all that terrible outback. Still missing.

'Of course you're leaving,' he said. 'You should have left yesterday when I told you to.'

Running frantic fingers through her hair, she tried to tame its tousled disarray. 'I'm not going anywhere, Mr McKinnon. I mean it. I have no plans to leave Mirrabrook. I'm here to find my brother and I'm not taking orders from anyone, especially from you.' She remembered something she'd learned during her conversation with Marsha. 'I understand you have a brother and a sister, so if you won't help me I'll talk to them. That's what I plan to do next.'

'Do you indeed?'

'Yes, I do indeed. I assume Tim had dealings with them as well as you?'

He shrugged. 'Not really and Annie's away in the city at the moment, so she won't be able to help you.'

She was determined not to be put off. 'I'm

sorry to disappoint you, but I'm not leaving.' Throwing off the sheet, she gripped the bedside table for support while she swung her legs over the edge of the bed and stood carefully. 'I have a strong feeling that I'm going to get the answers I need right here in Mirrabrook. I'm not budging until I get to the bottom of all this.'

The phone rang, cheating her of the opportunity to hear Kane's reaction to her brave little statement.

He snatched it up. 'McKinnon speaking... Oh, hello, Reid... Yeah, I'm still in town... No, I didn't have any luck, mate... There's no one available. Yeah, of course, I really tried.'

Over his shoulder, he scowled at Charity and she hurried to her suitcase, grabbed the first items of clothing she found and disappeared into the bathroom.

As she closed the door behind her, she heard Kane snap into the phone, 'What choice do we have? You and I will just have to manage on our own, won't we? We'll have to become New Age types and discover our feminine sides.'

In the privacy of the shower, Charity rested her aching forehead against the cool ceramic tiles and let warm water pour over her.

What was she going to do now? It was all

very well to toss off some grand sounding words to Kane about her plans to stay in the Mirrabrook district to search for Tim, but who would help her and where was she going to stay?

She wondered how much a cabin like this one would cost her. She didn't have much money and had been hoping to clear the problem up quickly.

When she emerged from the bathroom with her hair wrapped in a huge white towel, she was dressed rather inappropriately in the first clothes she'd grabbed—her best cream trousers and pale blue silk blouse. Kane had hidden his muscles beneath a cotton shirt and he was sitting on the edge of his bed, his expression morose.

'Is something wrong?' she asked.

'Just a stubborn brother.' He looked up at her and stared hard at the towel on her head.

She felt frozen by the sudden intense spark in his eyes.

'What's the matter?'

'I was wondering what colour your hair is when it's wet.'

Surprised and flustered, she said, 'I don't know. It's just red, I think.'

He stood and seemed to tower over her.

'No, not red, Charity. Your hair could never be *just* red.'

For a moment she thought he was going to reach out and unwind the towel. But he didn't. He just stood there and the intense way he looked at her caused a shivery pang—an empty hollow, deep inside her.

'I came out to find my hairbrush,' she said, sounding more panicky than she meant to. No man had ever looked at her with such un-smiling, focused attention. At home in Hollydean she'd had a few boyfriends—some unimpressive, others a little more serious. There'd even been a marriage proposal. But none of those men had made her feel so—so *aware*.

She dashed to her handbag, grabbed her hairbrush and hurried back into the bathroom, shutting the door behind her again.

Safely inside, she used the electric hair-dryer to blow her hair dry. At home she usually let her hair dry naturally, encouraging it to fall into soft waves, but today she didn't care if it went as straight as sticks as long as it stopped Kane McKinnon from looking at her *that* way.

The intensity in his eyes had awoken a strange longing deep inside her—a need so acute that it left her with the fear that it might never be eased.

Shocked by her reaction, she wound her flamboyant hair into a prim knot and secured it with several pins before she ventured back into the bedroom.

'Now you look like a Sunday school teacher,' he said, and she was relieved to see that his eyes were less intense.

'Perhaps that's because I *am* a Sunday school teacher,' she replied with necessary dignity.

'Fair dinkum?'

'Yes. I'm a genuine Sunday school teacher.'

He cocked his head to one side and studied her. 'What else do you do?'

What else did she do? Annoyed by the underlying taunt in his manner, she straightened her shoulders and lifted her chin to an even more dignified angle. If only she could offer this man an impressive answer. If only she could manage to lie without feeling guilty.

What else she did was less than impressive.

While most of her school chums had gone away to travel, or to university, or to jobs in London, she'd stayed behind in Hollydean to help her father and Tim. Whenever her friends came home, they took pains to point out that she'd been living in a time warp since she left school.

She knew Kane McKinnon wouldn't be impressed by the news that she played a vital role in the parish—taking care of the rectory household, accompanying the choir practice, teaching at Sunday school, visiting the elderly and the sick...

And it was of no use to point out to him that she was so indispensable to the running of the parish that the ladies in the Mothers' Union had organised themselves into a roster to take over her tasks while she was away.

Nevertheless, her green eyes flashed and she cast him a look ablaze with haughty pride. 'I am an excellent housekeeper,' she said.

His lips pursed as he released a low whistle. 'Are you now? That's very interesting...'

Letting out an impatient huff, she folded her arms across her chest. She'd had enough of his teasing. 'I seem to remember you mentioned breakfast?'

'That's right. I did. Are you ready?'

'I could be if I knew what you've done with my shoes...'

Bending down, he fished for something under the end of her bed, then he straightened and held out her sandals, dangling them by the straps. 'These do?'

'They'll be fine, thank you.' With icy composure she accepted them and slipped her feet into them, but she felt strangely self-conscious and fumble-fingered while he waited and watched her lean down to do up the buckles.

'Now I'm ready,' she said crisply.

'Good. Let's go down to the dining room.' He opened the door and stood aside to let her past. 'Once you've got some decent tucker inside you, we should have a chat. I've got a suggestion that might interest you.'

'*Your* housekeeper?'

The way she said the word *your* set Kane's teeth on edge. She might as well have come right out and said she'd be happy to take care of any other house on the planet—*except* his.

'It makes sense, doesn't it?' he said, spearing a juicy sausage with his fork then attacking it with his knife. 'If you're going to insist on looking for your brother, you need somewhere to stay, and Reid and I need someone to cook and do the housework.'

'It would probably do your brother and you the world of good to fend for yourselves for a week or two,' she said in a preachy voice that he supposed she'd perfected during her years as a Sunday school teacher.

'It would probably do your brother the

world of good if he was left to carry on with his life without his sister breathing down his neck.'

'You don't understand.'

'And neither do you.'

They scowled at each other across the table, green eyes and blue sparking with equal ferocity. Then Kane gave a resigned shrug and resumed eating while Charity pushed the food around on her plate. Apart from sipping daintily at her pineapple juice and nibbling at her toast, she'd hardly touched the rest—only a little of the mushrooms and tomatoes.

'You may as well eat up,' Kane said. 'A big pile of greasy food is good for a hangover.'

She looked ill, but he ate steadily on, relishing every speck of food on his plate—softly scrambled eggs, crisp bacon and sausages with tomato sauce, a lamb chop, mushrooms—

'Very well, I'll do it.'

Her sudden statement caught him by surprise. He looked up to find her watching him with a deadly earnest expression.

'I'll take the job as your housekeeper because it serves my purpose as well as yours,' she said. 'But I'm putting you on notice, Mr McKinnon. The only reason I'm coming out to your homestead is because I need accommodation and because I believe that someone in this district will be able to explain my brother's disappearance.'

'I can't promise you anything on that score.'

'I know you've tried to deter me, but that doesn't change my opinion.'

Kane shrugged. 'Suit yourself.'

'And I'll come to look after your home on the strict condition that you—' In mid-sentence her composure crumpled. A tide of colour swept up her neck and into her cheeks.

Not for the first time, Kane wondered how a clergyman's daughter could have such pagan prettiness. This girl's lissom figure, vibrant hair and dewy green eyes would distract any red-blooded man.

And now this rosy blush…pretty as a sunrise. A Sunday school teacher out of her depth shouldn't look so damn appealing.

His throat seemed to close and he had to swallow. 'What was that? You mentioned a strict condition.'

She took a sip of pineapple juice and looked at him over the rim of the glass and her eyes seemed to plead with him to understand.

'What condition?' he repeated.

She still didn't answer. But, as her blush deepened, Kane understood.

Pushing his plate to one side, he propped an elbow on the edge of the table and rested his chin on his hand. 'Perhaps I should explain *my* conditions,' he said.

'You have conditions?'

'Naturally.'

'Then by all means, please explain.'

'There are very few women I would ask to move into my home.'

Her eyes were huge and she nodded without speaking.

Leaning forward, he said quietly, 'Apart from Annie, there are no women living on Southern Cross. There's an old stockman who looks after the yard and he and my brother Reid and I are all bachelors—bachelors, living on an isolated cattle property.'

'Oh,' she said very softly and her pink mouth stayed in the shape of a circle.

'Three men and a pretty young lady living alone could start tongues yapping from one end of Star Valley to the other. A hint of scandal runs through this district like a bushfire. So it needs to be made clear right from the start that there must be no involvement of—how can I put this delicately?'

'You don't need to,' she cried. By now her

face was fire truck red. 'I understand perfectly and I wouldn't dream—'

Keeping his face solemn, Kane offered his hand to shake hers. 'Our arrangement is strictly business.'

'Oh, yes. Absolutely. That is *exactly* what I was trying to say.'

'Then it seems we're perfectly suited, Miss Denham.'

She looked as if she'd swallowed a grasshopper.

'Oh, and one other thing,' he said. 'Try to stay away from the gin while you're working for me.'

Charity fumed as she helped Kane load the back of his utility truck with stores. It had been completely unnecessary for him to spell out the need for propriety. And she knew that he knew that. Which meant that once again he'd been deliberately teasing her. And, indirectly, he'd also been making sure she understood that he didn't desire her.

As if that wasn't obvious! One look at Marsha had told her she would never be Kane McKinnon's type.

'I thought there was only yourself, your brother and one other man on Southern Cross,' she said as she carried a box rattling with bottles of various sauces and mayonnaise to the truck. 'Just how many will I be cooking for?'

She was stunned by the quantity of food Kane had ordered. Crates of oranges and apples, bags of flour, rice and sugar, a drum of olive oil, packets of pasta, boxes of tinned vegetables and fruit juice and crates of beer all had to be stowed away along with her suitcase.

'There will probably be just the three of us—plus yourself, at least for the first few days,' he said. 'But we have to stock up properly.' He took the box from her and stowed it next to a stash of toilet paper rolls. 'You can't come running back into town every five minutes.'

'I realise that.'

'There's always a chance that the fencing team we're expecting later in the month could arrive early,' he said. 'It depends on how their previous jobs pan out. But you could handle cooking for a few extras, couldn't you?'

'Of course.' She was determined to sound confident, no matter how many challenges this man threw at her. At least she was getting to Southern Cross where she'd be able to speak to Reid McKinnon. And perhaps in time she would find a way to get more information out of Kane. She was sure he hadn't told her everything he knew about Tim.

It was a pity his sister Annie had gone to the city; but Charity was sure that if she was patient she would find people in the district who were prepared to answer a few discreet questions.

Kane threw a tarpaulin over the load and began to secure it with rope. 'That should keep most of the dust out,' he said when he'd finished. He turned to her. 'Okay, that's it. Let's hit the road, Chazza.'

'I beg your pardon? Who's Chazza?'

He dropped his gaze to the dusty toes of his riding boots and grinned. 'Sorry, that just slipped out. We're an uncouth lot in this country. We do terrible things to names. Barry becomes Bazza; Kerry is Kezza. So you'll find yourself getting called Chazza. Or would you prefer Chaz?'

'Do you have a problem with my real name?'

'No. But I'm afraid nicknames tend to happen out here whether you like it or not.'

'Then in that case I'll take Chaz.'

'Chaz it is then.'

He grinned again, but her own attempt to smile faltered.

Australians were very in-your-face. Tim

had mentioned in his letters that the ringers liked to toss him teasing jokes to see how he handled them. No doubt it was their way of testing a newcomer. And as a new chum she was expected to throw one back.

Her brother would have been able to handle it. She, on the other hand, had always been too earnest to be good at witty exchanges.

She repeated the word Chaz softly under her breath and decided she probably liked it. Chaz. Chaz Denham. It sounded upbeat and trendy. She had never in her life been trendy. But no way would she admit to Kane that she quite liked the idea of being Chaz.

After she had climbed up into the passenger seat, slammed the door shut and buckled her seat belt, she said, 'I have to admit an old-fashioned name like Charity can be something of a burden. Tim is lucky he isn't my sister.'

'Do you think a sister might have been christened Faith or Hope?'

She rolled her eyes. 'Perhaps.' It was time to give him a taste of his own medicine. 'My father excelled himself when he chose my middle name.'

'Yeah?' An unmistakable spark of curiosity flashed in his blue eyes. 'What is it?'

'Chastity.'

His jaw dropped. 'You've got to be joking.'

For almost a minute he sat with one hand on the steering wheel and the other on the key in the ignition, staring at her, his expression cagey, as if he were sizing her up. Then a knowing smile dawned. 'This is payback time, isn't it, Sunday school teacher?'

'For the way you've teased me mercilessly all morning?'

'Rubbish. I've shown lots of mercy.'

'Forgive me for not noticing, Mr McKinnon.'

He grinned and turned the key in the ignition and as the motor revved he said, 'So are you going to tell me your real middle name?'

His arrogant assumption that she would tell him was so annoying—especially when he wouldn't tell her one measly thing about Tim. And, although it was trivial by comparison, the thought that he really wanted to know her middle name was exquisitely satisfying.

'Never,' she said.

CHAPTER THREE

THEY took off down Mirrabrook's main street, passing a little wooden church, the police station and the tiny post office, several shops and offices, a freshly painted café, and a larger modern building which housed the library and the *Mirrabrook Star*, the local newspaper.

Then followed a row of little timber houses with iron roofs, deep, shady verandas and front gardens bright with flowers, and suddenly gum trees crowded close to the narrow blue bitumen and the road plunged into bush again.

Shortly after that they came to a signpost pointing to Breakaway Station and Southern Cross Station and they took a dogleg turn off the main road and were rattling along a dusty and bumpy outback track.

Beneath a startling blue sky the stark landscape flashed past in a blur of brown and khaki streaks—dusty green foliage, grey-brown tree trunks and pink-red earth showing through a scant covering of dry grass. In the distance menacing mountains loomed, studded with black granite boulders. The Star Valley was nothing like the pretty valley Charity had expected. She didn't understand how civilised people could give this wilderness such a charming name. The valleys of her experience were pleasant green and grassy dips in a gentle English landscape, more like folds in a green velvet skirt.

Of course, she had known that a valley in Outback Queensland would be different from one in Derbyshire. Her brother's letters had told her about the vast and rugged outback, but somehow she'd never quite grasped how very vast and how exceedingly rugged it was.

And now, as she looked out into the rushing bush, she shuddered. It was into this wild, hostile wilderness that Tim had vanished. Seeing the inhospitable landscape for herself made his disappearance even more impossible to accept, too awful to believe. Where, oh, where was her fearless, daredevil little brother?

The truck hit a deep wheel rut and she was forced to clutch the door handle and brace herself with her feet against the floorboards. Why on earth had Tim been so eager to come to Australia? If she had had the chance to travel, she would have chosen to visit elegant

European cities like Paris or Venice, Vienna or Prague.

Not this endless bush.

She'd read an article on the plane that said Australia was twenty-four times the size of Great Britain—and Tim could be anywhere in this enormous country.

They travelled on and on over the winding dirt road, dipping down to cross rocky, dry creek beds, climbing out on the other side between steep red banks and then continuing across the plains till they reached yet another dry creek crossing.

What startled Charity most was that there were no signs of human habitation. And yet there had to be people somewhere because someone had placed a sign that said:

Beware
Cattle on the road.

And not far past that sign she saw a mob of strange-looking, droopy-eared cattle lying in the inadequate shade cast by dusty gum trees. The grass around them looked dead. 'How on earth do you raise cattle in this country?' she asked.

'Your British breeds don't do well here, but

we have Brahman cross cattle that are bred for
the tropics.'

'But what do the poor things eat?'

'Dried grass still has nutrients in it—a bit
like dried fruit for us, but we give them sup-
plements as well. The hard part is keeping
enough water for them. We have to pump water out of the creeks up into troughs. When
the dams and creeks dry up completely, we're
in trouble.'

'Living out here must be hard work.'

He shrugged. 'Who wants a cushy job?'

A well-paid cushy job was the goal of most
of the fellows she'd met. A cushy job, a pretty
little wife...

Apparently, Kane McKinnon wanted neither.

'Of course, you're seeing this country at its
worst—at the end of the dry season,' he said.

'Is it very different after rain?'

'You wouldn't recognise it.' After a bit he
added, 'We don't hold the cattle here for too
long. These properties are for breeding stock.
You wouldn't try to fatten them here. We've
shipped all our young beasts over to our other
property near Hughenden. With luck, they'll
fatten up nicely there.'

'They certainly couldn't grow very fat on
this grass,' Charity commented, but already

her thoughts were straying from the plight of cattle and back to Tim. Was *he* lost and starving? 'In England we often hear about people dying in the outback.'

'Yeah, it happens.' Kane stared ahead of him at the yellow track. 'This is a tough country, but the people who perish are usually folk who don't have a clue what they're doing and should never have left the city in the first place. Your brother was a quick learner and I'm sure he'd be okay in the bush.'

She turned to look out through the side window and saw a grey kangaroo hopping with an easy, fluid bounce-bounce-bounce as it made its way between the trees. It was her first kangaroo sighting, and she might have been excited if she wasn't so worried.

'What was Tim's state of mind?' she asked. 'Did he seem happy?'

'He was fine. Look, the one thing I like about your brother is his ability to keep to himself. He quietly got on with the job and he didn't have to be the centre of attention. He fitted in well out here. I'm sure he's still doing well wherever he is.'

Kane sounded so certain that Tim was fine that Charity wondered again if he knew more than he was letting on. Was he hiding the truth from her? She turned to study him. His eyes met hers and he sent her a quick, reassuring smile and she realised with something of a start that she wanted him to do it again. In that momentary flash of friendly warmth, the mockery had left his eyes and his mouth had softened and she'd felt a queer little kick in the stomach.

They stopped under the shade of trees beside a creek to drink from their water bottles.

'At least you'll be safe from Marsha out here,' Kane said as Charity took more tablets to keep her headache at bay.

She was surprised to hear him make such an ambiguous comment about his girlfriend. 'When will we reach Southern Cross?'

'We've been travelling on the property for the past half hour. Won't be too much longer now.'

She had no idea what to expect when they finally reached the McKinnon's home, but five minutes later they pulled up outside a tiny, tumbledown shack, and Kane jumped out of the truck and began to untie the tarpaulin covering the load in the back.

Her heart sank as she stared at the house. This was Southern Cross homestead? It was a sorry sight, crouching in a dusty paddock beneath a rusty iron roof, with a sagging front veranda and unpainted timber walls left to weather to a silvery-grey. And Charity started to question her impulsive decision.

Her headache returned as she pushed the passenger door open and stepped down into the dirt. The heat of the sun beat on to the back of her neck and her unsuitable clothes stuck to her. With every step, her feet picked up fine red dust that slipped between her sandals and the soles of her feet and caught between her toes.

Kane hefted two boxes of groceries from the truck and balanced them on his shoulders.

'Can I help?' she asked.

'Could you grab that box of tinned stuff?'

'Certainly.'

As she followed him into the hut the wooden front steps creaked ominously. A dog barked and she saw that a blue speckled dog had been tied up to one of the veranda posts.

'G'day, Bruiser,' called Kane. 'Is the boss home?'

The dog seemed to go back to sleep as Kane shoved the front door open with one elbow. Charity couldn't suppress a shudder as she followed him inside. Surely Kane's sister Annie couldn't be responsible for this untidy interior? The floors looked as if they hadn't been swept for weeks. An old coffee table was littered with beer cans, magazines and filthy ash trays. There were no curtains at the windows and a piece of fraying hessian had been tacked over one frame in place of glass.

The floor of the narrow passage leading to the back of the house was covered by cracked linoleum that looked a thousand years old. Kane carried the groceries through to the kitchen and dumped them on a rickety table before opening the fridge.

Charity gasped. 'It's full of beer!'

He sent her a withering glance over his shoulder. 'Blokes in the bush have to get their priorities right.'

'But what about your sister? How could she live here?'

Slamming the fridge door shut again, he turned to her and rested his hands lightly on his hips. 'I take it you're not too impressed with this place?'

Charity gulped. She couldn't bear the thought of living here, but her upbringing had made her excruciatingly tactful and she didn't want to hurt Kane's feelings.

His upper lip curled and his voice grew cold as he said, 'Maybe you don't have what it takes to look after a place like this.'

'I'll do my best,' she croaked. 'But, to be honest, I can't see much evidence that this house has been carefully looked after.'

He laughed then. Actually laughed. And she wanted to hit him. Her hands clenched and she drew in a sharp, angry breath. She was hot and headachy and worried about Tim and the thought of living in this messy, tiny, shabby hut was the last straw.

'Chill, Chaz,' he said.

'Chill?' she almost shouted.

'Calm down. This isn't Southern Cross homestead. This is an outstation, a camp the ringers use as a base when they're mustering. One of the guys has stayed on here, keeping an eye on this neck of the woods, and I'm just topping up his supplies.'

'For heaven's sake!' She glared at him. 'You can't resist teasing me, can you?'

'You left yourself wide open for that one.'

Again, she wanted to hit him.

'Sorry,' he said, but he didn't look the slightest bit sorry. 'I'm afraid I've been teasing Annie since she was knee high to a mosquito. It's a bad habit.'

'It certainly is. I feel very sorry for your sister and I'd appreciate it if you'd desist.'

'Annie has a good sense of humour.'

'Good for her. Mine disappeared along with my brother.'

That took the smug smile from his face.

Casting a quick eye over the kitchen, Kane

shrugged. 'It doesn't look as if Ferret's here, so I'll leave this on the table and we may as well keep going.'

'To Southern Cross?'

'Yes.'

The ringers' hut had shaken Charity's fragile confidence and as they continued their rattling journey along the dirt track that wound its way through more dusty bush she prepared herself for more disappointment. She supposed that if people lived in the middle of nowhere there wasn't much need to have a nice home to impress visitors, but she hadn't realised that outback people managed with so few creature comforts.

How did women like Annie McKinnon cope?

'This is our place coming up now.' Kane's voice broke into her thoughts. She peered ahead through the dusty windscreen and caught snatches of white and fresh green flashing between the trees.

Then they rounded a bend in the track and she saw iron gates painted pristine white and, beyond them, an expanse of green lawn flanked by lush palm trees and clumps of white bougainvillea, as pretty as bridal veils.

And then she saw Southern Cross homestead.

It was a huge, sprawling low-set house, built of timber painted snowy-white and wrapped around by deep, shady verandas. A garden of green shrubbery and white flowers fringed the verandas.

'Oh, how lovely,' she said, knowing she couldn't have been more surprised if she'd fallen down a rabbit hole and found herself in Wonderland.

'This place more to your taste?' Kane asked.

It was like coming across an oasis in the desert. 'It's fantastic.' Unable to contain her amazement, she asked, 'How do you manage to keep the lawn so green?'

'That's old Vic's job.' Kane nodded towards the tree-lined watercourse that had run parallel to the road for the last part of their journey. 'He pumps water up from the creek,' he said. 'But when the creek runs dry, we lose the lawn.'

'Does that happen very often?'

'Every few years we get a bad drought. If we don't get a good wet season this year, we'll be in trouble.'

He drove on around to the back of the house so that they could unload the stores directly to the kitchen pantry. As they pulled up a chorus of barking greeted them.

Dogs—a black Labrador, a blue and white spotted dog and a Border collie—came racing from several directions. Kane shot a sharp look in Charity's direction.

'Do dogs bother you?'

'No, not at all. I love them. We have a Border collie at home.'

She noticed, however, that the collie, after peering hopefully up at the truck, turned and retreated to the veranda where it lay with its head on its paws, paying them no more attention.

'That's Lavender,' Kane told her. 'She's Annie's dog and she always mopes if Annie goes away.'

'Oh, the poor thing.'

They climbed down from the truck. 'The blue-heeler cattle dog's mine,' he said. 'His name's Roo.'

'Hello, Roo.' She gave his speckled head a friendly scratch.

'And the Labrador's Gypsy. She's Reid's dog.'

'Oh, Gypsy, you're very beautiful.'

A wizened, sunburned fellow, bowlegged no doubt from years astride a horse, ambled around the side of the house, and Charity was introduced to Vic. He beamed at her when she complimented him on the beautiful garden.

'If you enjoy having flowers in the house, miss, pick as many as you like,' he told her.

'You'll have a friend for life if you keep feeding him compliments,' Kane said, as Vic left them. Then, with the greetings over, he ordered Gypsy and Roo to clear off. 'We've got work to do,' he told them. 'So give us some room.'

The dogs retreated happily to lie in the shade and Kane and Charity unloaded the truck. As they carried boxes of groceries through to the pantry room, Charity stole curious glimpses down hallways and through doorways to the rest of the house. She gained an impression of unexpected coolness and casual elegance—of very high ceilings and polished timber floors, antique furniture and beautiful rugs.

The last thing she'd expected was to be charmed by Southern Cross. What a pity she was so worried about Tim.

If she wasn't continually haunted by his disappearance she might have been able to enjoy working here.

Kane found his brother in the machinery shed, working on the diesel motor of one of the station's trucks.

'I've found us a housekeeper, so you don't have to worry about getting dishpan hands.'

Reid looked up and chuckled. 'I've been worried to death about dishpan hands.' He snatched a rag from a nearby bench and wiped black grease from his fingers. 'I thought you said there were no housekeepers to be found this side of the black stump.'

'Yeah, well, this one kind of fell into my lap.'

'Oh, no. She's not one of your fan club, is she?'

Kane grimaced. 'Give me a break. It's someone new to town and she happens to be looking for temporary work.'

'That's a stroke of luck. Is she experienced?'

'She's an English woman who's worked as a housekeeper for a vicar.'

Reid's face broke into a grin of approval. 'Sounds perfect,' he said and he gave Kane a congratulatory poke in the ribs with his elbow. 'So we can assume she's a good cook?'

Kane shrugged. 'I guess so. We'll find out tonight. I've let her in gently, so we're just having sandwiches for lunch—cheese and pickle. As a matter of fact, lunch is ready now.'

'Terrific. I'm starving.' Reid threw the rag

aside and together they left the shed and crossed the wide stretch of grass that separated the garage and machinery sheds from the main homestead.

The brothers were twins and of similar build, but that was where the similarity ended. Kane's sandy hair and blue eyes were more like their younger sister Annie's, while Reid's hair was darker and his eyes deep grey.

According to their mother, Reid was the older twin by a clear margin, and all their lives Reid had never let Kane forget it. He played the big brother role to the max.

'So what did you say this woman's name was?' he asked.

'Er—Chaz.'

'Chaz?'

'Yeah.' Kane swallowed and felt uncomfortably conscious of his brother's shrewd gaze. 'Chaz Denham. Charity Denham, actually.'

'Denham? Isn't that the same name as our young pommy jackaroo?'

Damn it. There was no way he'd be able to keep Charity's identity under wraps. Sooner or later Reid was going to find out. Charity had already threatened to question Reid about her brother. 'She's Tim Denham's sister.'

Reid came to a halt in the middle of the yard. 'What's she doing out here?'

'Looking for her brother.'

'Hell.' Reid frowned and shook his head. 'What have you told her?'

'I've told her that Tim could be anywhere.'

'You must know you're taking a big risk bringing her out to Southern Cross.'

'Well, I was sick of you bellyaching about wanting a housekeeper.'

'Come off the grass, Kane. You knew I wasn't desperate.'

Kane set his jaw at a stubborn angle. 'Could have fooled me. Anyway, she's safer out here than snooping around in Mirrabrook asking nosy questions.'

'I suppose that's true,' Reid said, but he shook his head as if he wasn't certain. 'What's she like?'

'She's—' Kane shrugged, not sure he could come up with a satisfactory answer. He glanced towards the back door and saw Charity standing there. 'See for yourself.' He nodded in her direction, then he held his breath, waiting for Reid's reaction.

It came in the form of a low whistle. 'Are you sure you know what you're doing, little brother?'

Kane flinched and felt sweat form under his collar.

Charity had changed into a sleeveless blue cotton dress and as she stood there, framed by the doorway, the sunlight set her brandy-coloured hair alight and her pale skin gleamed whitely and she looked like something an artist would want to capture on canvas.

She realised they were both looking her way and raised one hand to wave shyly and, although the gesture was innocent, there was something about the graceful flutter of her slim, white hand that made the movement intensely seductive.

'Just let me handle her and everything will be fine,' he told Reid—but he spoke with ten times more conviction than he felt.

There was no breeze to relieve the midday heat as they ate their sandwiches out on the veranda.

Charity hadn't planned to join the brothers for lunch, but they insisted. Reid McKinnon was charming and spoke to her very politely, with none of the teasing she'd come to expect from Kane. She was itching to ask him questions about Tim and nursed a small hope that if she could get him alone he would answer her questions more honestly than his brother had. But during lunch she was careful to only ask questions related to her responsibilities as housekeeper.

At the end of the meal, when the two men were about to leave, Reid turned suddenly to Kane. 'Have you kitted Charity out yet?'

Kane frowned.

'Take a look at her,' Reid said. 'She's a snowdrop, an exotic flower. Look at her colouring—milk-white complexion, light-coloured eyes, red hair.'

Kane's eyes met Charity's and she felt her cheeks grow warm. He was looking at her the same way he'd looked when he'd insisted that her hair could never be *just* red.

'The poor woman won't last a minute out in our sun unless you help her to dress properly,' Reid continued. 'See she gets whatever she needs from Annie's room.'

'Please, don't go to any trouble. I'm sure I'll be all right.' She wasn't enjoying the way this discussion was taking place as if she wasn't there.

'My dear,' said Reid in a fatherly tone. 'Believe me, you need more protection than that pretty dress. Annie's got wardrobes full of gear. I don't want to feel responsible if you're burned to a crisp, or if you go into a heat stress coma while you're working for us.'

Turning to Kane he said, 'Make sure she gets an akubra.'

Then he left them.

Kane sent her a lazy smile. 'Well, Chaz, I'd better obey big brother's orders.'

'I tried to bring suitable clothes,' she said. 'I brought a pair of jeans with me. And some boots.'

'Don't worry.' He nodded his head towards the hallway that led to the bedrooms. 'Come on. Annie's got plenty of things for you to choose from and I'd say you're about the same size.'

She followed him through the house. Unlike the neat guest room she'd been given, Annie's bedroom was loaded with personal knick-knacks and the accumulated clutter that came with years of living in the same place.

It was a large room with French doors opening on to a veranda. On a desk in one corner sat a computer and a happy hotchpotch of paper, pens, books and coffee mugs. Above the desk, a cork-board was covered with photographs of family, friends and pets, and there were faded pin-ups of movie stars and rock stars that had probably been there since Annie's teenage days, as well as scribbled notes and more recent cuttings from magazines.

Charity wondered why Kane's sister had gone to the city. She had gained the impression that Annie had taken off without much warning—but, apart from the fact that they'd been left without a housekeeper, the brothers didn't seem particularly concerned.

'Now, let's see what's here,' Kane said, flinging open a wardrobe door.

A gasp of surprise escaped her. She hadn't expected to see pretty after-five wear. 'When does Annie wear these?' she asked, touching her fingertips to the hem of a rose-coloured silk skirt.

'We have a social life in the bush, you know. Parties, balls...but these dresses aren't what you need right now.' Kane tried another door and this time found a row of long-sleeved cotton shirts. 'This is more like it. Take a bundle of these. You'll need to keep your arms covered.'

From the top shelf he drew a wide-brimmed felt hat and popped it on her head. 'How's that? Does it fit?' Holding the brim, he wiggled it a little. 'That seems pretty good,' he said.

'It feels fine. Thank you.'

He pointed to a set of built-in shelves. 'There are more jeans there if you need them. Help yourself.' Then he bent down and pulled a pair of boots from the bottom of the wardrobe.

'I don't need boots,' she told him. 'I brought some with me and they're fine for the outdoors. I climbed Mount Snowdon in them.'

'Then they're probably cold weather boots.'

'Well, yes...I suppose they are.'

'These will be better. They're riding boots made of kangaroo hide.'

'But I won't be riding horses.'

'Doesn't matter. Kangaroo leather is light-weight and breathes. These will keep your feet cool. Try them.' He grabbed a pair of cotton socks from a drawer and held them out to her.

This was the second time Kane had watched her put on shoes, and again Charity felt self-conscious. Which was perfectly silly. Anyone would think she was doing a strip tease—not something as mundane as trying on cowgirl boots.

But there was a disturbing expression in Kane's eyes as he watched. He almost looked as if it pained him to watch her—and yet he never once took his eyes away.

'They fit very well,' she said and, to her intense embarrassment, she blushed.

'You're in luck then.' His voice sounded strangely strangled. 'Okay, now we've got your gear sorted out, we can do a quick tour of the place so you can get your bearings.'

Quick was the operative word, Charity decided as he whisked her outside for a hurried inspection of the cool room, separated from the house by a covered walkway, the washroom, the machinery shed, the tack room and the home paddock.

Glancing across the paddock of bleached grass to a line of shady trees, he asked, 'Would you like to see the creek?'

'Yes, please.'

She rather fancied the thought of a creek. Perhaps it would be a place where she could escape for quiet walks in the shade beside running water.

Minutes later, she discovered that the creek was indeed pleasant. Quite delightful, in fact.

Under the protection of overhanging trees the air was much cooler and the water bubbled and chuckled over pretty, smooth stones. Huge boulders, worn down over the centuries, formed natural stepping stones, and there were soft green ferns and reed-like grasses on the banks and dragonflies and water beetles flitting across the surface of the clear water.

'This is lovely,' she said as they crossed a broad shelf of flat rock. It was reassuring to know that there were places in the bush that provided a cool, quiet haven with nothing but the chatter of birds and the ripple of water for company.

'Stop.' Kane's sharp command was barely above a whisper. His hand gripped her arm.

To Charity's mortification, she jumped as if she'd never been touched by a man. 'What for?' she cried, startled by the way his unexpected touch sent a shaft of electricity through her. She tried to pull her arm away from him. 'What are you doing?'

'Come back this way.' It was a crisp, no-nonsense order.

'Why?'

'There's a snake. *Look.*'

A snake!

Out of the corner of her eye, she saw a distinctly slithery movement. *Oh, God. Oh, help!*

The big black snake must have been coiled on a rock in the sun, but now it was moving, its head lifted and weaving from side to side.

'Come—' Kane insisted.

She was too busy panicking to hear further instructions. Wrenching her arm from his grasp, she leapt backwards and hurried across the rocks, needing as much distance between herself and the snake as possible!

A snake! She'd never seen one in the wild

before. She couldn't believe this was really happening.

Kane was beside her. 'Don't panic,' he said. 'It's not going to chase you. You're safe here.'

She stopped running and he placed steadying hands on her shaking shoulders. Her heart galloped as she looked back. The snake was stirred up, and its head was raised and hooded, cobra style.

Now that she was at a safe distance, she watched it in a kind of awestruck horror. 'What sort is it?' she whispered.

'A red-bellied black snake.'

Then the snake took off, hurrying away from them, and Charity found herself staring in fascinated amazement. Inside she was shuddering, but she couldn't help admiring its fluid grace as it slid across rocks and into a shallow rock pool.

'Is it dangerous?' she whispered, watching as the snake hurried up the far bank. In its eagerness to escape from them into the bush, it lost its purchase on the slimy rock for a moment, but then it recovered and continued on till it gained the safety of the undergrowth.

'By Australian standards, it's not the most dangerous snake,' said Kane. 'But it's among the world's top ten.'

She gasped. 'Top ten most deadly?'

'Yeah.'

'Oh, God.' She pressed a hand to her stomach.

His eyes flashed blue as he touched gentle fingers to her cheek and traced a line down her jaw to the centre of her chin. 'Are you okay?'

'Of course.'

He withdrew his hand and she took a deep breath and managed a minuscule smile. 'But thank goodness you were here. I would have died of fright if I'd been here on my own. I was thinking it might be nice to come down here to relax. But no way.'

'You'd be safe if you brought one of the dogs.'

She shook her head. 'Not this girl. How can you bear to live here, Kane? It's so isolated and hot and dangerous.' Right now she couldn't think of one good thing about the outback. Why on earth had her brother wanted to come here?

The light in Kane's eyes dimmed and his mouth grew hard as he looked away, down the creek. 'I can't possibly explain. It's one of those things you'll probably never understand.' His cool gaze flickered over her. 'Like my brother said. You're an exotic flower. You don't belong here, so it's just as well you don't need to stay for long.'

'Yes,' she said, but as they walked back to the house and she saw the blankness in his face she didn't feel lucky at all. She felt inexplicably sad and unbearably confused.

It was shortly before sundown when Kane returned from helping Reid in the machinery shed. He entered the house by a side veranda and showered, using the bathroom farthest from the kitchen. He didn't ask himself if he was avoiding Charity, or why he'd changed into stone-coloured trousers and a freshly ironed shirt instead of his usual jeans and T-shirt, but he was relieved to discover when he came into the kitchen that Reid had gone to the same trouble.

Reid took two beers from the fridge, handed one to Kane and nodded towards the oven. 'Something smells good.'

Kane agreed. The kitchen was fragrant with the aroma of spices and onions and other smells he couldn't quite pinpoint.

'Where's Charity?' he asked, flipping the top off his beer.

'Not sure.'

'I'm through here in the dining room,' she

called in her lilting English voice. 'Come on through. Everything's more or less ready.'

The brothers exchanged surprised glances and Kane followed Reid into the room but, after taking only two steps inside, Reid came to such a sudden halt that Kane almost ran into him.

The dining room looked ready for a party. The table was covered by a crisp white Irish linen tablecloth and was set with their best heirloom silver and gilt-edged china. There were lace-edged serviettes beside each place and, in the table's centre, a crystal vase filled with flowers.

Charity didn't seem to notice the stunned looks on their faces until Kane spoke. 'You didn't tell us you'd invited the Prime Minister to dinner.'

She frowned. 'Is this more formal than you're used to? I wasn't sure what you wanted.'

'We usually just eat in the kitchen,' Reid explained. 'Unless there's a celebration, or we have guests.'

'Oh, what a pity.' She looked dismayed. 'You have so many beautiful things and I've had so much fun using them.'

'Never mind.' Reid flashed her his warmest

smile. 'It will be delightful to eat in here for a change, won't it, Kane?'

'Delightful,' Kane echoed and he might have smiled too, if he wasn't so annoyed by his brother's Prince Charming act. At lunch Reid had been full of concern for Charity's complexion and now, when she indicated the merest smidgen of disappointment, his brother was turning himself inside out to put her at ease.

Next minute he'd be offering to help her find her brother.

'Please, take your seats and I'll get your dinner,' she said, returning Reid's smile with one that was equally warm.

It wasn't until the men were seated at the table, with the aromatic casserole dish set in front of them and their beers transferred from brown stubby bottles into tall crystal glasses, that they realised there were only two places set.

'What about you, Chaz?' Kane asked. 'Aren't you joining us?'

'Oh, no.'

'Why not? Don't you trust your own cooking? You haven't added a dash of hemlock, have you?'

'No, it's not that. I'll have some later—in the kitchen.'

'No, you won't,' Kane insisted.

'But I'm the hired help.'

'Don't talk rubbish. This isn't England. We don't stand for that nonsense out here.'

'But Vic isn't eating with you.'

'Vic is different. He has his own cottage and likes to do things his way. Besides, he always joins us on Sundays.'

When she continued to look unsure Reid turned on the charm again. 'Charity, you're here as a stand-in for our sister. Kane and I insist that you join us.'

'Very well then,' she said, hurrying to the sideboard to find silverware for herself.

Still piling on the charm, Reid hurried to pull out her chair and he sniffed appreciatively when she lifted the lid from the casserole dish. 'This meal smells sensational.'

Show pony.

'I hope you like it,' Charity said and Kane fancied he saw a flash of tension in her eyes.

'I'm sure we will,' said Reid smoothly.

She ladled spoonfuls on to plates and passed them around, and Kane found himself watching her movements rather than the food.

She had the loveliest hands he'd ever seen—delicately boned, with translucent skin, slim fingers and neat, unpainted pink and white nails. He was transfixed; everything she did looked so graceful and dainty.

Heat surged through him as he imagined her hands touching his skin...

'What do you call this dish?' he heard Reid ask.

'Curried lentils,' she said.

'Lentils?'

Lentils? Kane came back to earth with a thump and stared at the food on his plate. He darted another quick glance at the rest of the food Charity had brought out—a bowl of salad and a newly baked loaf of bread. 'Will there be meat to go with this?' he asked.

'Oh, no.'

'No?' repeated Reid weakly.

'Why not?' asked Kane.

'I don't cook meat.'

'Why not?'

She smiled sweetly. 'I'm vegetarian.'

Kane gaped at her. 'You're what?'

'Last year my father and I gave up meat for Lent and we haven't eaten it since.'

'You went to all this trouble with the table setting and you serve us lentils?' Kane turned to Reid, who was staring at his plate. 'We haven't given up meat, have we, Reid?' When his brother didn't answer, Kane spun back to

Charity. 'Why didn't you tell me you were vegetarian?'

'You didn't ask.'

'But, for crying out loud, you can't expect us to go without meat just because you have.'

'Calm down, Kane.' Reid spoke in his smoothest, most diplomatic voice. 'Charity, you do understand that we make our livelihood from *beef*, don't you?'

'Oh, yes,' she said, smiling.

'And, as far as I know, eating meat is not exactly a sin,' prompted Kane.

Reid made soothing noises. 'We can discuss this later. One meal of lentils won't hurt us.'

It had better be only one meal.

Although Kane wouldn't admit it, the lentils tasted good. Bloody good. And the bread Charity had baked and the dressing she'd made for the salad were delicious too.

Across the table his eyes met hers. She smiled and he fancied he saw a cheeky gleam lurking in the depths of her smile. He found himself needing to look at her again and again. Each time, he thought he caught an impish spark, before she quickly lowered her gaze.

As the meal progressed, he grew more and more certain that this whole situation—the excessively formal dining setting and the humble meal of lentils—were Charity's payback for the way he'd teased her about the ringers' hut that morning.

And, to his immense surprise, he found the thought that Charity was playing games with him far more satisfactory than he should have.

CHAPTER FOUR

She'd lost Tim.

It was the week before Christmas and she was in London, in crowded Oxford Street... dodging busy shoppers. Her mother was inside Selfridges, buying Father's favourite imported cheese and it was Charity's job to look after Tim. But she'd been distracted by the beautiful Christmas displays in the shop windows and her brother had escaped from her. He was such a wicked little monkey; he'd laughed back at her as he disappeared into the crowd. She'd searched three blocks and she couldn't see him anywhere.

Mother would be devastated when she found that she'd lost him...

What could she do? She couldn't bear to see her mother's lovely face distorted by heartbreak...

A telephone rang shrilly and Charity woke with a start. Her heart thumped. Phone calls in the early hours so often brought bad news. Could it be news about Tim?

Struggling to throw off her dream's stranglehold, she saw the pearly-grey light of dawn seeping into her room and she remembered that she'd come to Southern Cross.

Before she could scramble out of bed, she heard the sharp rap of boots hurrying along the hall and Reid's deep voice answering the phone, but she couldn't hear any of the conversation and Reid hung up quickly and hurried away again. She lay there, listening to his fading footsteps…worrying…wondering.

Then from the other side of the house she heard the rumble of male voices, and guessed that Reid and Kane were discussing the call. She wondered if she should get up and start making breakfast, but Kane had said that six o'clock was early enough and it was only a little after five, so she decided to stay in bed.

Even at this early hour it was a warm, still morning. She lay with only a sheet covering her, studying her room in the mauve morning light. On the dresser there was a photo in a copper frame of a laughing, blonde-haired, blue-eyed girl hugging a Border collie. The girl bore a marked resemblance to Kane, so Charity decided she must be Annie. She looked rather nice.

Why had Annie gone to the city? For an assignation with a boyfriend?

It was understandable that Kane's sister would want to take off for the city. She looked like the kind of girl who needed fun and friends...boyfriends. Maybe that wasn't possible when she lived way out here in the bush.

Her thoughts were interrupted by a bird calling loudly from outside her window. Sitting up, she drew the curtain aside and saw a blackbird perched on the veranda railing. He was rather handsome with his black coat and snowy-white tail and golden eyes. As she watched, he threw back his head and called again and it sounded for all the world as if he were saying *Hello, Hello*.

And then she heard more footsteps and the back door slamming and moments later the growl of an engine revving. Through the window she watched a truck coming around the side of the house and driving off away from the homestead. She couldn't see the driver, so she had no way of knowing whether it was Reid or Kane.

Did it matter?

She admonished herself for hoping that it wasn't Kane taking off somewhere without speaking to her. How silly. If it was Kane who had driven away, she should be pleased. It meant she'd have an opportunity to speak to his nice brother about Tim. It was very possible that Reid would be more prepared to tell her the truth. He was a gentleman.

Unlike Kane.

Rolling over, she closed her eyes. It wasn't worth going back to sleep, but she tried to relax...tried not to think about Kane...

She wasn't falling for him. Of course she wasn't.

She wasn't the kind of girl who fell in love in five minutes and she certainly wasn't the kind of girl who was attracted to external qualities like shiver-sexy eyes and strapping muscles.

She could only love an admirable man. At the very least she needed a man who was honest, a man she could trust. Which ruled out Kane McKinnon. Completely.

'Don't tell me you're cooking bacon for breakfast? Not bacon *and* eggs?'

'Oh, it's you.' Charity whirled around from the stove, egg-flip in hand.

Kane's eyes widened. 'Who were you expecting?'

'I heard someone drive off. I thought perhaps you'd gone away.'

'That was Reid. We had a phone call from Mick Rogers, the manager of our property near Hughenden. His wife had a baby last night.' Kane didn't look particularly happy about the news.

'Is everything all right?'

'We hope so, but the baby's premature, so she and her mother have been flown into Townsville and Mick wants to be with them.'

'That's understandable.'

He nodded. 'So Reid's going over to take care of Lacey Downs.'

'Has he already gone?' She felt a rush of panic.

'Yes. We have weaner stock we moved over there a few weeks ago and he wants to keep an eye on them.'

'How long will he be away?'

His eyes narrowed as he frowned at her. 'Hard to say. Depends on how things go with the baby.'

'I wish I had known he was leaving,' she said. 'I didn't get a chance to talk to him.'

Kane seemed tense from top to toe. He eyed her warily. 'What about?'

'Tim, of course.'

He shook his head. 'He wouldn't have been able to tell you any more than I have.'

Which is a big fat nothing.

She had the good sense not to say so aloud. 'Reid left without having any breakfast.'

Kane grinned. 'He'll survive. He'll grab a

bite to eat at a café in Charters Towers.' He
peered over her shoulder at the food in the
frying pan. 'So you've managed to rustle up
a non-vegetarian breakfast.'

She made a show of rolling her eyes at him.
'I made a superhuman effort.'

'Believe me, Sunday school teacher, I'm
deeply grateful.' His smile lingered knowingly
as she piled his plate with bacon and eggs and
he carried it to the kitchen table.

When he was settled, she asked, 'What are
your plans for today?'

'Reid's asked me to check out a problem
we're having with stock getting out into the
back country. There must be a fence down
somewhere.'

'Will you be gone all day?' She was annoyed to hear disappointment creeping into
her voice. Had Kane heard it?

'I'd say so.' Kane paused in the process of
cutting bacon. 'I hope you don't mind being
here alone. You'll have old Vic, of course,
and I'll leave Roo behind. Lavender won't
budge from the back steps, so you'll have two
guard dogs to protect you.'

'Yes, of course. I'll be fine,' she said, but
she spoke more bravely than she felt. Crumbs,
she would be alone out here in the middle of
absolutely nowhere with an old man and a

couple of dogs. Her hand shook slightly as she poured tea from a big brown teapot into two mugs.

Watching her tremble, Kane frowned. 'You *will* be okay, won't you, Chaz?'

'Of course.' She would look on Reid's and Kane's absences as blessings in disguise and make the most of her solitude. If she found old Vic she could discover what *he* knew about Tim.

'If there's any kind of emergency, ring zero-zero-zero,' Kane said. 'That'll get you straight through to Emergency Services.'

'I'm sure there won't be a problem.'

'No, but forewarned is forearmed.' He pointed his knife towards her empty plate. 'You're not eating.'

'I should be making your lunch, so you can take it with you. What would you like? Will sandwiches be okay?'

'There's no rush. Have something to eat before you keel over.'

She grabbed a slice of toast from the toaster and began to spread it with marmalade.

For a while they both ate and drank their tea in silence.

As Kane drained his second cup, he said, 'Whatever you do, don't talk to strangers while I'm gone.'

'Heavens, Kane, are you trying to frighten me?'

'No, of course not.' Nevertheless, a grim wariness settled over his features as he looked at her.

How ironic. One minute she was dreading the thought of being alone and now she was frightened by the idea of confronting a stranger.

'What kind of strangers am I likely to meet out here? There's no one for absolutely miles.' She stared at him in panicky puzzlement.

'Most people telephone ahead and let us know when they're coming for a visit, so if anyone turns up here out of the blue—let Vic deal with it.'

'Okay,' she said, but she didn't feel okay at all.

'Just be sensible,' Kane said.

'Don't worry.' She was proud of the super-brave smile she managed. 'I'm exceptionally sensible. I've had oodles of practice at being sensible. It's been expected of me all my life.'

'A sensible little Sunday school teacher.'

'Exactly.'

She expected to see another of his teasing smiles, but his eyes shimmered with a strangely puzzled expression as if he was planning to ask her another question. But then he frowned and shook his head as if he'd had second thoughts.

He rose to his feet. 'I'd better make tracks.'

'If you call back in here before you leave, there'll be sandwiches and a thermos of tea ready for you.'

He smiled. 'Thanks, Chaz. I'll let Vic know what's happening and I'll be back to collect the lunch in fifteen minutes.'

When Kane took off on his motorbike, disappearing in a cloud of white dust into the bush, Charity experienced a moment of pure panic.

She was alone now.

Hurrying to the back door, she found Lavender and she plumped down on the step beside her and hugged her. 'You poor old thing. I know just how you feel. We've both been abandoned, haven't we?' She rubbed the dog behind her ears. 'Our dog, Barnabus, loves to be rubbed like this. You'd like him. He's incredibly handsome.'

Lavender pressed a wet nose against Charity's cheek, making soft, grateful doggy noises. 'We're in the same boat, Lavender. You're waiting for Annie to come home and I'm waiting for news of Tim.'

Roo came running up to them, his tail wagging and his eyes alert. 'Do you think you're missing out?' she asked and she hugged him too, and let him lick her face. But, despite the canine company, she felt homesick and horribly lonely.

But she had to snap out of it. She was perfectly safe with two dogs and a gardener for company, and there was a telephone if she needed outside help. And Kane had only gone for a day.

Which meant she had one day to find out what the gardener knew.

'Young Tim? Yeah, I met him. He was a nice young fella.'

Ensconced in a comfortable cane chair on the homestead veranda, Vic smiled at Charity as he reached for another of the jam drops she'd baked.

At first he'd been taken aback when she'd asked him to join her for morning tea.

'I don't usually stop for smoko,' he'd said, but one mention of jam drops and he hadn't needed a second invitation. 'Haven't eaten these in years,' he said, dunking his biscuit into his tea.

'Have as many as you like.' Charity pushed the plate closer to him. 'So tell me more about Tim. Did he seem happy?'

'He was having the time of his life, love. Settled into the outback like a mosquito in a swamp. Happy to work from sunup to sunset.'

'That makes a change. He always dodged the washing-up at home.'

Vic grinned. 'The life of a ringer is like no other on earth—primitive conditions and lots of hard work, but time for fun too. And you can't beat camping out under the stars.'

'I guess not.' She could imagine what a big adventure it must have been for Tim. 'He didn't happen to tell you where he was going when he left here, did he?'

Vic opened his mouth to say something, but thought better of it.

'Please don't hold back,' she urged him. 'I'm so worried. If you can think of anything that might give me a clue. It just doesn't make sense that he took off without telling anyone his plans.'

'Are you absolutely certain he's missing?' Vic asked.

She frowned. 'Yes, we haven't heard from him in over a month.'

He mumbled something and shook his head.

Charity set down her teacup and saucer and leaned forward, watching him. 'What is it, Vic?' The old fellow seemed uncomfortable,

as if he were battling an urge to tell her something he either didn't want to, or knew he
shouldn't, tell her.

'What has Kane told you?' he asked at last.

She sighed. If she admitted that Kane had
told her nothing of any use, the old fellow
would probably clam up. 'Kane said that Tim
worked here on a mustering team and that if
I could find someone he'd befriended on the
team they'd probably be able to tell me where
he planned to go next.' It wasn't quite the
truth but it wasn't exactly a lie.

Vic frowned. 'Have you met anyone else
from the team?'

'Not yet.' She tried to sound casual. Picking
up her cup again, she drank more tea. 'What
can you tell me, Vic? I've come all this way
and I must find Tim.'

'All the way from England,' he said and
sighed as if the very thought of all that travel
made him tired.

'Yes, and I promised our father I'd find him.'

'Well…'

Charity leaned closer.

'I can tell you that Tim's all right,' he said.

'Yes…but what else?'

He sat in silence and reached for another
jam drop.

His answer was the same as Kane's. *Tim's*

all right. What did these men mean by *all right?* They were so darn secretive. 'How do you know he's all right?'

But the old fellow shook his head and got stiffly to his feet. 'Can't sit too long or my old joints seize up,' he said.

'But Vic, what about Tim? Why can't you tell me?'

'If Kane wanted you to know anything—' He stopped in mid-sentence.

'You mean Kane knows more than he's letting on?'

Vic looked worried. 'You should trust him. Look, I've got to go, miss. Sorry I can't be of more help.' He shuffled backwards away from her. 'Thanks for the morning tea.'

She'd scared him off. Vic was in so much of a hurry to get away he left a half-eaten jam drop on his plate.

Charity frowned as she watched him disappear around the side of the house. If Tim was all right, why was there so much mystery? Why couldn't someone jolly well come out and tell her where he was?

And if Tim *really* was all right, why hadn't he let his family know?

After gathering up the morning tea things, she went to the laundry room to deal with a load of washing and, as she worked, her imagination played with possibilities. Could Tim be doing something he didn't want her or Father to know about?

She thought of Marsha. Was Tim having a passionate affair? Surely he was too young.

The heat was blistering by the time she finished hanging washing on the clothes-line and she was immensely grateful for the protection of Annie's wide-brimmed akubra and long-sleeved shirt. Even so, her body was slick with sweat. It gathered under her collar, at her waist and between her breasts.

She couldn't imagine what it would be like to be out in the scalding sun and the dust all day, as Kane was, hunting down lost cattle and mending fences.

After lunch, she stood at the sink washing the few things she'd used. A fly buzzed and butted at the insect screen, but she was only dimly aware of it as she stared, mesmerised by the heat haze that shimmered over the paddocks, and the blue-green fuzz of bush that spread beyond it.

Already she was getting used to this sun-burned landscape. She supposed that given time she could discover all sorts of things about the bush that were invisible to her now.

Lost in thought, she took some time to recognise a throbbing roar in the distance.

When she realised it was Kane's motorbike returning, a hot wave passed through her body. The bike appeared suddenly in a flurry of dust, zooming out of the line of scrub, across the home paddock, and coming to a stop near the simple structure of metal sails mounted on a tall metal tower that served as a windmill.

Roo bounded up to greet Kane as he dismounted and he bent down and gave his dog's ears an affectionate scratch. Then he took his boots off, set them aside and pulled a lever on the windmill and water gushed from a pipe a few feet above him.

She hadn't meant to stare, but somehow she couldn't drag her eyes away. Backlit by the sun, the water flashed with golden flecks as it splashed over Kane's head and shirt. She imagined how good it must feel for him to wash all the dust and heat away and she stood transfixed, watching every movement, every detail.

Within seconds the thin fabric of his shirt turned transparent and moulded to his frame. He dropped his head back to let the water course over his face and in his hair.

Oh, man. She'd been in a dither yesterday morning when she'd seen Kane without a shirt, but that had been only half as breathtaking as seeing him in a *wet* shirt. The tapering line from his shoulders to his hips was perfection. And now wet *jeans* were added to the equation.

It was a sight beyond perfection.

It was enough to make a girl hyperventilate. Greek statues in the British Museum had *nothing* on a drenched Kane McKinnon.

And it just kept getting better. Next minute, Kane was hauling his shirt off and washing it beneath the spilling water and Charity watched the mouthwatering way his muscles rippled beneath his smooth, bronzed, *wet* skin.

This *had* to be a life enhancing experience.

Roo danced and yapped at his master's feet and Kane filled his hat with water and bent over to let the dog drink from it and Charity was absolutely certain she'd never seen anything quite so fascinating. Thank heavens there was no one around to tell her she shouldn't just stand there gaping.

No female could be expected to turn away.

Eventually, Kane turned the water off and began to walk towards the homestead, carrying his wet shirt, boots and hat. When he reached the back veranda and draped his shirt over the railing, Charity was still standing at the window clutching a tea towel to her bosom.

'Hey, Chaz,' he called. 'Any chance of a cold drink?'

Oh, crumbs. Had he seen her ogling him? Cheeks flaming, she dashed to the refrigerator.

She hurried on to the veranda, carrying a tray with a glass and a jug of iced water and lemon slices. 'Is water okay?' she asked. 'Would you rather have beer?'

His face split into a broad grin. 'No, water's fine.'

She set the tray on the top step beside him and stepped back quickly. Behind her back, she pressed her thumb and finger together to stop the bleeding from the cut she'd scored from slicing the lemon too quickly.

Kane ignored the glass and, sitting on the step, drank straight from the jug. His Adam's apple worked in his throat as he drank and Charity felt as if she'd been pumped full of steam from head to toe.

She'd tried not to draw comparisons between this outback cattleman and the neat, pale fellows she'd dated; had tried to remind herself that she didn't trust Kane McKinnon. His physique was merely the result of lucky DNA. She was shallow to be impressed by such things.

What counted was a man's honourable heart. His *honesty*. Muscles signified nothing. *Nothing*.

Then again, how important was an honourable heart when any minute now she was going to explode into a thousand pieces?

'Shall I get you a towel?' she asked him.

'No, thanks.' He set the almost empty jug back on the tray. 'With this hot breeze blowing I'll be dry in no time.'

'It's a very hot day.'

'Yeah.' For a moment he closed his eyes and relaxed his big shoulders against the veranda post, taking long, slow, deep breaths.

His chest rose and fell with the rhythm of his breathing and Charity was very unwilling to leave and yet uncertain she should stay. His lashes were dark against his cheek, his mouth in repose soft and…

His eyes opened slowly. 'So how was your morning, Chaz?'

'Fine,' she said, trying desperately to look as if she had reasons for remaining glued to the spot—reasons that had nothing to do with his bare torso. 'What about you? Have you finished your work?'

'Yeah. I found the problem with the fence and it was quite easy to fix. Didn't take as long as I thought it might.'

'That's good.' She hunted for something else to say. 'I invited Vic up for morning tea.'

Kane grinned. 'He would have loved that.'

'Yes. He appreciated my jam drops.'

'Jam drops? You made jam drops?' The look he sent her reminded her of a boyish Tim when he'd come home from school, ravenous. 'Are there any left?'

'Yes. Would you like some?'

'You bet.'

She flew back into the kitchen and returned with a plateful.

'These are terrific,' he said, munching. Then he frowned. 'Don't stand to attention like a servant waiting for orders. Take the weight off your feet.'

Too shy to sit beside him on the step, she leaned one hip against the veranda post. 'I'm comfy here.'

He ate two jam drops and reached for another. 'Annie will never forgive you if you spoil us rotten.'

'I'm curious about your sister,' she said. 'Does she help with the cattle, or does she just look after the housework?'

'When she was younger she used to love helping with the cattle, but in recent years she's lost interest. These days she tends to read a lot. She subscribes to magazines and book clubs and she's always on the Internet.'

'If it's not too prying, may I ask why she's gone to the city?'

Kane shrugged. 'I don't know exactly. I imagine she's having a bit of a city fix—going to the movies and shopping—gossiping with girlfriends. Most of her school friends live in Brisbane now.'

'Wouldn't you like to know for sure why she's gone?'

'Not really. She's not a teenager any more. I'll probably ring this evening for a bit of a chat.' He reached for another biscuit. 'These are good. You're a great cook, Chaz.'

She decided that at least one of them should be brutally honest. 'I should admit that I had an ulterior motive when I baked these for Vic. I wanted to talk to him about Tim.'

In an instant a shadow darkened Kane's face. He looked away, staring out across the parched home paddock. 'I told you not to worry about your brother.'

She released her breath in an impatient huff. 'That's impossible.'

Avoiding her gaze, he grabbed his wet shirt from the veranda rail. 'I'd better take these wet things to the washroom.'

Here we go again, she thought, deeply disappointed. More evasions. Surely that meant he was hiding something.

'Kane, what do you and Vic mean when you tell me that Tim's all right? Why can't you tell me how you *know* he's all right?'

'Don't hassle me about it now,' he muttered.

'What's wrong with now? You don't look particularly busy.'

'Give it a miss, Charity.' His tone carried the weight of dark anger.

'How can I trust you if you won't tell me anything?'

'If you can't trust me, there's little more I can do.'

'So you refuse to talk about Tim?'

'I have nothing more to say.'

The heat lingered into the evening, but Kane's manner was cool. No more teasing. No easy banter. He didn't even seem particularly pleased that Charity had cooked him Beef Bourguignon, although he thanked her politely. After the meal he disappeared into his office to do paperwork.

Charity telephoned her father. She had to fight off an urge to weep when she heard his dear, familiar, very English voice. She tried to make her news sound positive, and told him that she was enjoying herself and that she had leads on Tim and that everyone in the district was confident he was fine. It was simply a matter of tracking him down.

Father, bless him, didn't ask awkward questions.

Afterwards, she chose a paperback novel from a bookshelf in the lounge and took it to read in bed, but lay thinking about Kane instead...about how he made her feel...and how she wished with all her heart that she could trust him.

When she eventually fell asleep, she dreamed...

'I'm home, Mother.'

Shoving open the stiff back door, she charged into the rectory and dumped her school bag on the kitchen floor. Friday afternoon! The whole glorious weekend stretched ahead. The house was filled with the welcoming smell of baking and she saw a perfectly golden berry pie and mouthwatering jam drops set on cooling trays beside the stove.

'Mother?' she called when there was no answering response. 'Mother, where are you?'

Still silence.

She went through to the lounge.

Her mother was— Oh, God, no— She was lying on the floor in the middle of the room, with one arm out-flung and her mouth slack, her lips deathly pale.

NO! No! No, Mummy! No! No-o-o!

Sobbing and screaming, Charity somehow remembered to run to the telephone.

But then she fell into a dark pit of horror until ambulance officers came rushing through the front door carrying a stretcher.

'Have you tried to resuscitate her?' a big, red-faced man demanded.

'No,' she sobbed. 'I didn't know how.'

If only she'd done that first aid course at school.

Shaking his head at her, the man ignored her terrified tears as he helped the other officer to carry her mother away.

Next day she saw the stranger.

Kane was gone again. He told Charity at breakfast that he would be away for most of the day. This time he didn't offer an explanation and she couldn't help feeling that he was deliberately avoiding her. Avoiding her annoying questions.

Midmorning, she was working in the front rooms, dusting and polishing the beautiful old furniture, plumping up cushions, changing the water in vases and rearranging flowers, when, through a window, she saw a man in a black, wide-brimmed hat crossing the lawn and scurrying around the side of the house.

Kane's warning had frightened her and, with the remnants of her nightmare haunting her, the sight of this stranger sent her stomach churning and lifted hairs on the back of her neck.

The stranger seemed to appear out of nowhere, without any visible form of transport, and there was something distinctly creepy and furtive about his manner.

Charity stood very still, hardly daring to breathe, wondering what she would do if he came into the house. Where was Vic?

She heard Lavender's low bark and then a man's syrupy voice sweet-talking the dog into compliance. Then silence. Did Lavender know him? She'd gone very quiet.

A knock sounded at the back door and although Charity had been half-expecting it she almost jumped out of her skin. There was no way she would answer the knock. If this fellow really wanted to talk to someone he could go and find Vic.

She felt ill as she stood there, frozen with fear, her ears straining, waiting for the sound of his footsteps walking away, but all she could hear were sounds from outside—the soft swish of the garden sprinkler and the rusty creaks of the old windmill out in the paddock as its sails turned slowly.

Then came the dreaded snap of the screen door being unlatched at the back of the house. And footsteps.

Inside the house.

Terrified now, she tried to think of somewhere to hide. Hurriedly she yanked off her elastic-sided boots, then waited until she heard the intruder go into the kitchen before she hurried in her socks across the hall into the nearest room—Annie's.

Without a second thought, she opened the door of the built-in wardrobe and squeezed inside among Annie's party dresses, pulling the door closed again.

She tried not to panic, but her breathing sounded shockingly loud in the confined space. Her heartbeats were thunderous as the heavy footsteps continued, moving from room to room through the house, sometimes muffled by carpets, then ringing loudly again as they crossed timber floors.

Her mind whirled. Who was this man? Why had Kane suspected that something like this might happen?

Was any of this connected to Tim's disappearance?

Oh, help, she couldn't think about Tim or she would give in to total panic.

When he came into Annie's room she stiffened, rigid as a broomstick, and held her breath. A tulle frill on one of Annie's evening dresses tickled her nose. Terrified that she might sneeze, she turned her head slightly and a coat-hanger bumped against the door. Oh, sweet Lord, had he heard?

She prayed as she'd never prayed before.

The intruder took for ever to examine Annie's room, shuffling papers on her desk, opening drawers...

Was there something inside the wardrobe that she could use as a weapon to defend herself if he found her? All she had were her boots.

It felt like ten weeks passed before he left, moving on to the next room... And it was ages before he left the house... Another half hour before she crept to a window and saw him skulking off, leaving Southern Cross the way he'd come, vanishing into nowhere.

She waited thirty minutes more before she felt safe enough to go out of the house and she dashed straight to the gardener's cottage.

'Vic!' she cried, hammering on his door. 'Vic! Where are you?'

When there was no reply she almost panicked. But then Roo came bounding up to her, his eyes alert, ears pricked sharp, barking loudly.

'Where were you when I needed you?' she scolded him. 'Off chasing wallabies? Some guard dog you are.'

He jumped up at her, then turned and began to scamper away, but then propped and looked back at her and barked again.

She frowned. 'Do you want me to follow you? What's up?'

The dog took off, bounding across the paddock towards the windmill and Charity hurried after him.

She found Vic slumped on the ground beneath the windmill with his back propped against one of the tower supports. His face was pale and drawn and his arm was twisted at a freakish angle, and Charity knew immediately that it must be broken.

A smothering cloud of panic descended. This was her worst nightmare.

For the past twelve years she'd feared this moment—when she would face another medical emergency. She'd dreaded it. Despite their family doctor's reassurance that there was nothing she could have done to save her mother on that fateful Friday—that the heart attack had occurred long before Charity had come home from school—the awful guilt lingered.

*   *   *

'What happened?' she asked Vic, crouching down beside him and hoping he didn't realise how terrified she felt.

'I'm not sure, love. I was up on the tower, trying to find what was blocking the pump, and something gave way and I fell.'

Her stomach lurched as she pictured him falling all that way. 'Are you hurting anywhere besides your arm?'

'I got a few bumps and bruises, but me arm took the brunt of the fall. I reckon it's broke.'

'I think it is, Vic.' She was pleased that she sounded calm. 'Look, stay here while I go and ring Emergency Services. The number's zero-zero-zero, isn't it?'

'Emergency Services? Don't ring them.'

'Why not?' Her voice turned squeaky as panic threatened again.

'It's only a broken arm. Not a real emergency. We don't want to tie the ambulance up and bring them all the way out here for a little thing like a broken arm.'

A *little* thing? The poor man had to be in a great deal of pain.

She took a deep breath. The truth was that she knew exactly what she must do. She'd done countless first aid courses over the past twelve years, desperately hoping that she would never have to use any of the knowledge she'd gained. 'I can make you more comfortable and put your arm in a splint, but you need proper medical attention.'

'Yeah, I'll need to get into Mirrabrook to see the doc.'

'Right.' Sitting back on her heels, she looked at him. He was trying to be brave. Heaven knew how long it would be before Kane got back. 'Don't worry, Vic, I'll drive you to the doctor's.'

'You know how to manage a four-wheel drive ute?'

'No,' she admitted. At home she zipped around quiet English lanes in a little automatic car. Here she would have to drive a ute with floor shift gear changes and there was the treacherous road that she would have to contend with. 'But I'll manage it with a little coaching from you.'

She couldn't let herself think about the miles and miles of terrible rough track she would have to drive over. One thing at a time. 'Now, let me help you into a shadier spot and then I'll make you some nice sweet tea and find something to splint your arm.'

'Thanks, love. You're an angel.'

CHAPTER FIVE

WAS this *déjà vu*?

Kane stared at the rectangle of white paper propped against the sugar bowl in the middle of the kitchen table. Only days ago Annie had left a note like this. And now Charity. Had she run away too?

Anxiety kicked like a boot in his gut as he snatched up her message and read it.

Balling the paper, he hurled it in the direction of the sink.

'Bloody hell!' he yelled into the empty house as he dashed to the telephone and began to dial frantically.

He barked his name as soon as there was an answer and then, 'I believe my housekeeper is on her way into town with Vic Mattocks. He's had an accident.' His fingers drummed on the desktop.

'Oh, hello, Kane.' Marion, the woman who doubled as nursing sister and receptionist for Mirrabrook's doctor, spoke calmly—but then she was trained to be calm, no matter what the crisis.

'Can you let me know as soon as they reach you?'

'Actually, Vic's here. He arrived some time ago.'

Thank God. Charity must have made it safely over that rough dirt road. The massive pressure constricting his chest began to lift. He could breathe again. 'How's Vic?'

'Fine now. Dr Gifford has just finished setting his arm, but we're going to keep him here overnight.'

'Good idea. What about Miss Denham?'

'Is that Charity? The young Englishwoman?'

'Yes. Can I speak to her?' He needed to tell Charity to stay in Mirrabrook overnight too. She could take a room at the pub and book it up to him.

What she mustn't do was try to come home now. Most likely she didn't know how quickly the sun set in the tropics—even in summer. She wouldn't make it before dark and it was far too dangerous for her to try to negotiate the track at night.

'I think she's already left,' Marion said.

'Oh, hell, no.' Apart from Charity's inexperience on outback roads, there was the danger of hitting a kangaroo or stray stock in the dark. God, the very thought of her having an accident drenched him in a cold sweat. 'Can you check? If she's still there, tell her to stay in town.'

'Just a minute and I'll check for you, Kane,' she said, her voice as calm as ever.

'Thanks.'

His fingers drummed another impatient tattoo until Marion returned.

'Kane, are you there?'

He realised he'd been holding his breath. 'Yeah, sure.'

'I'm afraid I can't find Charity. It seems she's already left. She told Vic she wanted to try to get back to Southern Cross before dark.'

Silently, Kane cursed. 'When did she leave?'

'Only about ten minutes ago.'

'Vic can't have been thinking straight. He should have warned her she can't possibly make it here before dark!' Realising how loudly he'd roared, he was instantly apologetic. 'Sorry, Marion. I hope I didn't burst your eardrum.'

'I'll recover.'

'It's just that I hate the thought of a girl fresh out from England trying to take on that track in the dark.'

'Charity seems very sensible, Kane. Dr Gifford was very impressed with the splint she put on Vic's arm. I'm sure she'll drive very carefully.'

'But she doesn't know *cooee* about driving in the bush.'

Even driving at dusk was dangerous, with shadows flickering across the track and the setting sun jumping out in unexpected places to blind you.

Marion chuckled softly.

'What the hell's amusing you?' he demanded.

Now it was her turn to apologise. 'Sorry, Kane. I was just thinking that it's about time.'

'About time?' What the blue blazes was she talking about?

'Charity's an exceptionally pretty young woman, isn't she?'

'What's that got to do with anything?'

'A great deal, I should imagine.' She chuckled again. 'Give us a call in the morning and we should be able to let you know when Vic will be ready to come home.'

'Yeah, right.'

'Stop worrying and have a good evening, Kane.'

'You, too.'

After he had slammed the phone down

Kane stormed through the house to the front veranda. Standing on the top step, he glared out across the expanse of bush, his eyes straining for the sight of a vehicle. Which was pretty damn stupid considering Charity had only left Mirrabrook ten minutes ago.

He pictured her trying to drive into the setting sun. There'd be a thousand shadows camouflaging the ruts in the dusty white track and there'd be kangaroos appearing out of the scrub without warning. And she was alone, damn it.

What if the ute broke down? What if she got herself bogged in sand...or if she misjudged a jump up...or took a wrong turn in the dark...?

Anything could happen.

In his mind he saw an image of her lying injured and a raw kind of panic sent his heart racing. He'd never felt like this before. His stomach churned and his throat felt choked by something crazily close to tears. He had no flaming idea what the hell was the matter with him.

But one thing was certain. He couldn't stay here. Doing nothing.

Spinning on his heel, he raced back through the house, out through the back door. Reid had taken one ute and Charity the other, so he headed for his motorbike.

Charity was tired. Too tired to be facing the most frightening driving experience of her life.

She'd had a cup of coffee and some sandwiches at the café in Mirrabrook while the doctor set Vic's arm, and for a while the caffeine had given her a boost, but now the strain of her day was taking its toll. She hadn't completed half of the journey home yet and she was beginning to doubt she could make it.

The trip into Mirrabrook had been bad enough. The track was totally unpredictable. Sometimes sandy and at others deeply rutted, it had plummeted into rocky gullies when she had least expected it and she hadn't been able to relax for a moment.

What had made it worse was knowing that Vic, poor fellow, had been feeling every jolt like a knife thrust in his injured arm. At least he was comfortable and well cared for now.

But she still had this long journey to make. And the gathering shadows bothered her. The low angle of the sun sent spears of sharp, red light slanting through the trees to play tricks on her eyes. Her tired eyes.

Southern Cross was still an hour away. It

would be pitch-dark long before she reached it. And there were no street lights, no guide posts—just endless scrub and trees crowding close to the road and a winding, treacherous track with wheel ruts and sandy bogs and rocky creek crossings.

She wondered where Kane was. Would he have returned home by now? Had he found her note? She hadn't mentioned the creepy intruder in the note she'd left him. She hadn't wanted to sound panic-stricken, so she'd simply assured Kane that she had Vic's accident in hand.

But now the stranger's sinister stealth returned to haunt her. And the disturbing coincidence of Vic's accident and the stranger's appearance sent fear crawling over her like spiders.

She began to feel truly frightened. She was alone on this deserted track with night encroaching and somewhere out there in the bush the menacing stranger lurked.

And a sixth sense told her that somehow that man was connected to Tim's disappearance.

Concentrate on the road. The worst of it was that she couldn't be sure Kane would be there when she got home. *Don't think about that now.*

A shape leapt out from the shadows at the side of the road and she jumped in her seat and screamed as she slammed on the brakes. The ute came to a screeching, shuddering stop as a long-legged grey kangaroo bounced straight in front of her. Good grief. She'd almost hit it.

The kangaroo seemed unharmed and bounded away into the scrub on the other side of the road, but she was a mass of nerves. A trembling mess. And she'd stalled the ute.

She sat shaking, trying to pluck up the courage to restart the motor and to edge the ute forward again. If only she could pull into a friendly roadside service station.

Then she saw a single light dipping and bobbing some distance away and she wasn't sure if she should be glad or scared. Was it a headlight? A torch? Friend or foe?

Very soon she heard the throb of a motorbike engine.

Kane? Could it possibly be Kane? *Please, please...*

It was so close to nightfall now that she couldn't make out the driver's identity until the bike pulled up beside her. When she saw it was Kane she sobbed aloud with relief. Throwing the driver's door open, she almost fell out on to the road.

And with perfect timing Kane jumped from his bike and caught her.

Then his arms were around her, holding her close. Instantly protected. She felt a white-hot rush of relief and happiness. She was so grateful she had to fight off an impulse to cry. Heavens, anyone would think Kane had saved her from extreme danger, pulled her back from the brink of a cliff.

'Are you all right, Chaz?' His voice sounded strangely gruff.

'Yes.' With her eyes closed, she leaned into his chest, his beautiful, strong, reassuring chest.

'Thank God,' he whispered.

She felt the warm touch of his hand cradling her head and close beneath her ear she could hear the beat of his heart. Oh, man. She had a crazy urge to rub her cheek against the soft cotton of his shirt, to feel the smooth glide of his skin through the thin barrier of fabric. If she turned her face, her lips would actually touch the place where his shirt opened...

She could imagine it all...Kane taking her into his arms, like this...kissing her... Oh, yes, a kiss would be so...

No.

What was she thinking? *Not* like this. *Not*

Kane. She wasn't about to start kissing a man she didn't trust.

Besides, he had no intention of kissing her. He was simply making sure she was okay.

Disappointing reality settled over her like a strait-jacket and she stiffened. At the very same instant she felt Kane let her go. His hands slid down her arms, till their only points of contact were his fingertips at her elbows.

And, slowly, Charity came back to earth. To the reality that she and Kane were standing in the middle of a lonely bush track with the last of the light falling out of the day…while mosquitoes buzzed around their heads. It seemed as if eons had passed since she'd panicked and stalled the ute.

'I almost hit a kangaroo,' she said.

'It's hard to see them at this time of day.' He hooked a wing of her hair behind her ear and her stomach flipped. 'Thanks for taking care of Vic.'

'I managed the drive into town, but—'

'You've been brilliant, Chaz. Absolutely brilliant.' He smiled and placed two hands on either side of her face and dropped a quick, warm kiss on to her forehead.

There—she'd had her kiss—the kind he might have given his sister, Annie.

'You look done in,' he said. 'But don't worry. I'll take over the driving now.'

'What—what about your motorbike?'

'I'll run it up into the back of the ute.'

Turning away from her, Kane moved with the easy speed of an athlete as he unhitched the ute's trayback and swung it down to form a ramp. Then, to Charity's astonishment, he jumped back on to his motorbike, revved the motor and rode it up the steep ramp and on to the back of the ute.

While he was securing the bike she scrambled into the passenger seat.

It was quite dark now. Through the windscreen she could see the evening star shining in a purple ink sky above a line of black treetops.

Kane swung into the driver's seat beside her and in no time they were bumping along the track towards Southern Cross.

'Thank you so much for coming to find me,' she said.

He murmured something incomprehensible and then asked, 'So how did Vic break his arm? Did he have a fall?'

'Yes, I think he was trying to fix the pump on the windmill.'

In the dim light she saw his frown. 'The pump was working fine yesterday.'

She took a deep breath. 'Yes—but there was a stranger snooping around the place this morning, Kane. He was there for ages.'

Kane's hand bashed the steering wheel hard as he muttered an oath. 'Sorry, Charity, but I'm so mad. What happened? What about the dogs? Didn't they chase him off?'

'They didn't react much at all.'

He frowned and looked more worried than ever. 'It must have been someone they've met before. Did this person speak to you?'

'No. I don't think he saw me at all. I hid in Annie's wardrobe.' In spite of the fright she'd had, she smiled at him through the dark.

'Good girl.' He fell silent, as if lost in thought, then he said, 'I'm sorry you've had such a rough day.' She sensed the quick turn of his head as he looked at her. 'You've had a tough introduction to life in the bush.'

'Baptism of fire?'

'And you couldn't have handled it better.'

As they continued on he sat in thoughtful silence, his eyes on the road, and Charity didn't press him to discuss the stranger. She was terribly tired and for now she was content to be safe in the ute, rattling along the track, watching the moon float behind the clouds and the trunks of the trees flare silver in the head-lights and then recede into the black night.

But she could never feel completely secure or safe. Not when she was still sure that Kane was keeping secrets from her. Secrets that involved Tim.

In her mind she replayed the brief moments when he had held her. Had she imagined it, or had he enfolded her against his heart as if he cared—truly cared for her?

She sighed. What did it matter? At some stage very soon she was going to have to confront Kane and demand to know what was going on. She needed some straight talking about this stranger and about Tim. In fact, after her trip into town, she'd thought of a drastic plan of action that she was prepared to carry out to get the important answers she needed. But that could wait till morning.

At breakfast next morning she said, 'I've been meaning to ask you the name of the big black bird that wakes me up in the morning.'

What a chicken-hearted wimp! I've got to stop beating about the bush. Ask Kane. Now. I deserve to know exactly what's going on.

'It's probably a kurrawong,' he told her.

'Kurrawong. I guess that's an Aboriginal name, is it?'

He nodded. 'Kookaburra, kangaroo, wallaby, kurrawong—they're all Aboriginal names.'

They lapsed back into silence as they finished their meal.

What's the matter with me? Why am I avoiding the issue? Am I frightened I'll find out that Kane isn't the man I want him to be?

Jumping to his feet, Kane took his dishes to the sink. 'By the way,' he said. 'I've suggested to Vic that he should stay in town for a bit. He's getting on in years and he could do with a proper spell to get over the shock. That was quite a fall.'

She paused in the process of wiping the kitchen bench tops. 'You won't go away again and leave me alone here, will you?'

He shook his head. 'Not a chance.' Then he frowned. 'I've been out to check the windmill. I'm afraid it was sabotaged.'

'Oh, heavens.' A chill snaked through her as she thought of the intruder. 'Have you called the police?'

To her annoyance, Kane acted as if he hadn't heard her question. He released a long sigh and stood with his hands on his hips, staring at a spot on the floor.

'Kane?'

'I should never have brought you out here,'

he said. 'You should have gone back to the coast when I told you to.'

Crunch time. I can't let Kane avoid the truth again.

Still holding the damp dishcloth, she crossed her arms over her chest and sent him her very best icy glare. 'I'm very glad I didn't let you talk me into going away,' she said.

He must have heard the coldness in her tone, because his head jerked up and the quick glance he sent her was decidedly guarded.

'I know Tim's disappearance has to be connected with this intruder.' She drew a deep breath—for courage. 'It's time to come clean, Kane. You have to tell me what's going on, or—'

He stood very still, his eyes expressionless. 'Or what?'

She gulped. 'Or I'll force you to tell me.'

'And how do you plan to do that?'

'I'll speak to the editor of the *Mirrabrook Star*.'

'Charity, for crying out loud. Don't talk rubbish.'

'*Rubbish?* You think that's *rubbish?*'

When he began to shrug her question aside she lost her cool.

'What about all the rubbish you've been feeding me?' She threw her arms into the air, sending the dishcloth flying, scattering crumbs. 'Tim's okay, Chaz. Trust me, Chaz. Don't ask questions. Jump inside wardrobes if strangers come around, but don't expect any explanations.'

Without giving him a chance to respond, she rushed on. 'I might be an English chick. I mightn't know diddly squat about the outback, but I know that I deserve to be treated like an adult and not a naive, stupid little girl. If you insist on keeping me in the dark, you'll force me to go public with this. If *you* won't answer my questions, I'll get the press to ask them for me and then perhaps there might, at last, be a proper search for Tim.'

She stopped because she'd run out of breath.

Kane didn't move or speak as she stood, panting, bubbling over with fury.

Their eyes fought a silent battle across the kitchen. Cool silver-blue versus heated green. Then Kane dropped his gaze. He bent over slowly, scooped the dishcloth from where it had landed on the floor, and straightened just as slowly.

Balling the cloth in one fist, he looked at her again. At last he said, 'There's no need for such drastic measures. I'll prove to you that your brother is safe.'

She felt a hot rush of adrenaline. 'Are you serious?'

He nodded.

'You mean I'll be able to see him and speak to Tim?'

'Yes.'

A wave of emotions swamped her—astonishment, joy, confusion. She sagged against the bench, almost winded by surprise. 'Why now? Just because I threatened to go public?'

'No, because things are getting out of hand and it's got to a point where I can't leave you here on your own. I can't avoid having you involved any more.'

Her heart began to thud loudly. She felt breathless. 'So where is Tim?'

'I'll take you to him. It'll mean a long, rough drive through the bush.'

'That's fine. I don't mind.' Anything, *anything*, would be fine if it meant finding Tim. 'When?'

'Today. Now.'

Her mind buzzed with a hundred questions.

Kane glanced at his wrist-watch. 'In fact, we shouldn't waste time.'

'Right.' She took a deep breath, trying to adjust to this sudden, startling change of pace. Her other questions would keep for later. 'Just tell me what to take and I'll get everything ready.'

He cracked a tiny smile as he tossed the dishcloth into the sink. 'We should only need food and water.'

'And a first aid kit?'

'Yes, but we always have a first aid kit in every vehicle. There are a few other things you need when you head off into the outback. I'll write you a short list of the supplies we'll need.'

As she rinsed the cloth and squeezed the excess water from it, Kane grabbed a pen and paper from near the phone and sat at the table to scrawl a hasty list.

'If you can throw these things together that would be terrific. I'll find us a couple of back-packs,' he said.

'Backpacks? Will we be hiking?' Desperate as she was to find Tim, she wasn't sure she could keep up with Kane if they had to walk for miles and miles through the bush. Not in this heat.

'We can take the ute most of the way. There's only a short walk at the end.' Kane handed her his list. 'Don't let me forget to grab extra fuel.'

'Sure.'

He headed out of the kitchen but paused in

the doorway and turned, his hand gripping the lintel. 'Hey, what do you know?' He sent her a cheeky wink. 'I just worked out your middle name.'

'Oh, yes?'

'Gingersnap.'

'Gingersnap?'

'Sure. After that outburst, it suits you perfectly.' With that, he disappeared.

What outburst? She'd been perfectly reasonable. About to chase after Kane and tell him so, she was distracted by the sudden shrill ringing of the telephone.

'I won't let him get away with *Gingersnap,*' she announced loudly as she stumped back to the kitchen bench and lifted the receiver.

'Hello, Southern Cross station.'

'Marsha here, Charity.'

'Oh, hello.' *Lousy timing, Marsha.* She wasn't in the mood for a cosy chat with Kane's alcoholic girlfriend. 'How are you?'

'I'm peachy. I bet you are, too. I'm ringing to congratulate you on scoring such a crash-hot job on Southern Cross.'

'Thanks…' *I think.*

'How are you settling in?'

'Quite well, thank you.'

'I hear you've had some drama—something about a mercy dash into town with old Vic.'

'Yes, but the poor fellow was very brave. I know he was in a lot of pain, but he hardly flinched.'

'And someone said that Reid's gone over to Hughenden?'

Kane had been right when he'd warned her that gossip spread in the outback faster than fire. 'That's right. There was an emergency over at Lacey Downs and Reid's had to take over.'

'So—you're sitting pretty. Talk about luck! All alone on the property with Kane!'

Charity huffed an irritated sigh. 'I don't think that marks me as particularly lucky.'

'Try pulling the other one, Charity. A pretty Englishwoman way out there with Kane McKinnon. You'd be such a novelty for him.'

'You've got it all wrong. Kane's not the slightest bit interested.'

'I bet.' Marsha snorted her disbelief. 'He's put the hard word on you, hasn't he?'

Glad that no one could see her face, Charity refused to demean herself by answering this.

'If he hasn't he soon will. And you can't tell me you haven't thought about hitting on him.'

Charity sighed—again—extravagantly. 'Was there something else you wanted, Marsha?'

'Nice try, Charity. You *have* noticed that he's cut, haven't you?'

'Cut?'

'You must have checked out his six-pack—all those muscles.'

'Oh, the muscles—um, yes, I suppose he's well-built, but—'

'But nothing. I bet you want to jump his bones.'

For pity's sake! What could she say? Feminine pride prevented Charity from confessing that Kane had established house rules to cover such matters.

'Marsha, I promise you've nothing to worry about.'

'Yeah, right.'

Charity could imagine the way Marsha was rolling her eyes to the ceiling. It would be a waste of breath to try to explain to a woman like Marsha that she didn't make a practice of jumping into bed with a man just because she fancied him. An admission like that from a twenty-first century woman was like admitting to some deep misbehaviour.

'You really don't need to worry, Marsha. I'm not going to try to steal your precious Kane from you.'

From the passage outside came the sound of Kane's returning footsteps. 'I'm rather busy now. I have to go. But Kane's here. Perhaps you'd like to speak to him?'

'No. I won't bother him. Just give him my best.' Abruptly, she hung up.

'Who was that?' Kane asked as he came into the kitchen.

'Marsha.'

'What did she want?'

'She wanted to make sure I wasn't jumping your bones.'

Kane jerked as if an electric current had passed through him. Instead of regarding her with his usual mocking amusement, there was a flash of silver-blue alarm in his eyes and she saw his Adam's apple slide awkwardly in his throat.

'Don't worry, Kane. I reassured her that we have a strictly business deal.'

'You don't have time to gossip with Marsha,' he said gruffly. 'What's more important now is that list I gave you. I hope you've got everything ready.'

CHAPTER SIX

THIS time, as they took off through the scrub, there was no track to guide them, at least none that Charity could see. The steering wheel spun in Kane's hands as the ute crash-tackled the undergrowth and dodged between granite rocks, red anthills and gum trees. She sat with her heart in her mouth, overawed by his driving skill and his obvious, intimate knowledge of the terrain.

She wondered how long it took to understand this rugged, almost primal landscape. A lifetime? She was secretly pleased that already she was beginning to notice subtle things she'd overlooked when she had first arrived.

Her secret passion was art and, although she'd had little time to discover whether her interest sprang from real talent or just a love of art, she liked to view the world with an artist's eye.

She'd been interested to discover that all gum trees were not exactly the same. Some had smooth pink trunks while others were rough and reddish-brown, or dark grey. And the leaves varied too. Some were round and silver, while others were thin and tapered, pink-tipped or dusty-green.

And down by the creeks there were huge gums with majestic silvery-white trunks and crowns of delicate, lacy leaves.

Even the earth changed colour. The track was hardly ever just plain brown. It ranged from sandy white or grey to yellow or pink and deep, rich red.

After twenty minutes or so of their journey they topped a rise and before them stretched a flat, open, red soil plain, flanked on the far horizon by a solid, blue-green mountain range that stretched as far as she could see.

'We're heading for those hills,' Kane told her. 'That's the Seaview Range. It's part of the Great Divide that separates the inland from the coastal plain.'

'Is Tim there? In those mountains?' Excitement fizzed through her at the thought that she was going to find Tim today. Soon.

Kane didn't answer immediately. 'Be patient, Chaz,' he said at last. 'I'll put you in the full picture when the time is right.'

Be patient? Charity didn't know if she could bear more secrecy. 'Why can't you tell me now?'

'It's probably an unnecessary precaution, but I still think that the less you know the better.'

Her jaw dropped. 'Am I supposed to find that comforting?'

'Just trust me for a little longer.'

Her loud sigh was deliberately melodramatic. 'If this was a movie I'd have a gun pointed at your head, Kane McKinnon, and I'd force the information out of you.'

To her surprise, he laughed. 'Now you're starting to sound like my sister. Annie's always trying to imagine her life as something bigger and more dramatic than it is.'

'Well, if she's stuck out here with only you and Reid for company I can't blame her.'

She hadn't meant the comment to be hurtful, but she saw the laughter drain from Kane's face as if someone had pulled plugs from the soles of his boots.

'I mean—' she said quickly, hoping to make amends '—it must be hard for her without any other women around. She must long for a little, you know, girl talk.'

'She has plenty of girl talk on the Internet.' After a bit he added, 'But I know what you mean. Annie misses our mum.'

His voice grew gentle as he said this.

She said, 'I have to admit I've been curious about where your parents might be.'

'Our father died six years ago and Mum stayed on Southern Cross for about a year afterwards, but she was very depressed so we talked her into going back to Scotland to visit her sister.'

'Did she like Scotland?'

'Loved it. She was only going for a few weeks, but then it turned into a few months and she was so much happier over there that she ended up staying.'

'No wonder Annie misses her. Scotland's a long way away.'

'Yeah. Annie and Mum stay in touch, of course. They spend a fortune on phone calls.'

Charity stared out at the dusty plain. It was covered with anthills that looked for all the world as if a mad potter had run about creating strange, conical, terracotta sculptures.

She thought of her own mother. She'd been fourteen when her mother had died—that bewildering age when a girl needed her mother most. Neither Father nor Tim could ever make up for her loss. *I would give anything to be able to talk to Mother on the telephone. Just once.*

But she would become hopelessly maudlin if she thought about that now.

'You said you were going to phone Annie the other night. How is she?'

He grimaced. 'I didn't have any luck. There was no one home. She and her girlfriends must have been out on the town.'

'So you've had no contact with her at all since she left?'

'No.'

A glance his way told her that he wasn't quite as cool about this as he'd been earlier.

'Reid hasn't been able to get hold of her either,' he admitted. 'But he's going to put through more phone calls today until he tracks her down.'

She was relieved to hear that but she refrained from saying so. Kane would hardly appreciate it if she started fussing about his sister as well as her brother.

'Tell me a little about you and Reid,' she said. 'You must be close in age.'

He nodded. 'About as close as it gets. We're twins.'

That was a surprise. 'You don't look alike.'

'No.' He grinned. 'Most people think Reid's older, but that's because he was born first, and he's always taken his role as the big brother very seriously. He's been merciless with me since we were about six months old.'

'Oh, rubbish. I can't believe that. He's a perfect gentleman.'

Kane rolled his eyes. 'With ladies, perhaps.'

One mention of *ladies* and Charity remembered Marsha's phone call and she couldn't help saying, 'I hope you follow your big brother's good example.'

As soon as that comment was out she wished she could grab it back. Talk about sticking her nose into other people's business!

But luckily Kane didn't seem to hear her. They were descending into a creek bed and, unlike most of the creeks they'd crossed, this one had quite a lot of water flowing, so he had to concentrate hard on his driving.

He stopped the ute and changed the wheel-locks into full four-wheel drive mode and then began to inch the vehicle forward again. The water was almost deep enough to come through the doors. Plumes of white spray sheered out on either side of the vehicle and the ute's heavy wheels wobbled over slippery, water-worn rocks.

Charity held her breath, terrified by the loud scrape and bump of rocks against the underside of the vehicle. The ute's wheels seemed to sink into the finer gravel and she was sure they were about to go down to their axle—bogged for ever in a ute filled with water.

But at last Kane revved the motor and edged them out of the creek and up the steep red bank on the other side and, as they crested the rise, she saw the wide plains stretching ahead of them once more.

The ute sped forward again and Kane turned to her, his blue eyes dancing. 'That was just to keep you entertained. I thought the trip was getting a tad boring.'

'How very thoughtful of you.'

'Now what were you saying—just before we hit that creek?'

Heat flashed in her cheeks. 'It doesn't matter. I've forgotten.'

'Wasn't it something to do with my behaviour with women?'

'It was silly. Forget it.' She stared hard at a bunch of white clouds floating in the blue, blue sky. They were shaped like the British Isles. 'I—I'm not really interested.'

'You know the answer anyway.'

She stiffened. 'Of course I don't.'

'But I've been a perfect gentleman with you.'

She risked a glance his way. At that very moment their gazes met, and the amusement in his eyes was replaced by something else. It was almost imperceptible, but she saw a softening—an unmistakable message shimmering within the silver-blue and it caused a clamouring inside Charity.

It made her long to close the gap between them. To curl beside him and drop her head on to his shoulder. To have him touch her again. To kiss.

Her vision blurred and she blinked and when she looked at him again his eyes were back to the front, concentrating on his task. Had she imagined the way he'd looked at her?

'Of course you've been a gentleman,' she said, struggling to pick up the thread of their conversation. 'I—I wouldn't have expected otherwise. Not after our business agreement.'

Oh, cringe. Could he hear regret in her voice? Could he tell that she'd been having very *un*-businesslike fantasies about him?

She would never find out because at that moment the motor started to splutter. Kane cursed and suddenly red lights started flashing on the dashboard.

He braked sharply. The motor coughed and crackled, then stopped.

He cursed again.

'What's happened?'

'The oil pressure's gone,' he said. 'And the flaming engine temp's in the red.'

He looked so worried she felt a chill of alarm.

'Can you fix it?'

Kane didn't answer. Without another word, he jumped out of the ute and lifted the bonnet. She heard another curse. And then she smelled heat. It seemed to be coming from the motor—the unmistakable smell of heated metal that took her straight back to her schooldays, when she used to travel by bus past the foundry on the outskirts of Hollydean.

Quickly she clambered out of the ute and hurried to Kane's side. The motor was crackling and popping and the blast of heat was so overpowering she had to jump back from it.

'The motor's bloody cooked,' Kane said. 'I can't understand it.'

'How does it cook? Has it overheated?'

'Yes. Because we've lost all the oil.' He shook his head, clearly puzzled. 'I'm going to check underneath.'

His confusion bothered her. He'd seemed to be such an expert bush driver and she knew that he and Reid were experienced mechanics. Vic had told her that they kept all the vehicles and the pumps on Southern Cross in excellent working order.

Moments later, Kane rolled back out from under the truck, knocking red dust from his clothes and hair. 'It's the sump plug—for the engine oil. It's gone and so has all our oil.'

'But you carry spare oil, don't you?'

'Of course. But it's too late for that. Somehow the plug has unscrewed and we've had a sudden and total loss of engine oil. That's why the motor overheated.'

'Will you be able to get it to start?'

'No.' He dragged a dusty sleeve over his face. 'The motor's—jiggered—stuffed completely. I can't put it any more politely than that. It's useless. We'll have to get this damn vehicle towed back to Southern Cross and have a complete engine refit.' He kicked at one of the tyres. 'I've never heard of a sump plug unwinding itself completely—not even on the roughest roads.'

'That last creek crossing was pretty rugged.'

'That might have loosened it up a bit, but we would have had a slow leak and it would have shown up on the oil pressure gauge. Then I could have checked for the leak—fixed it up, topped it up with spare oil and Bob's your uncle. But I never got a chance to do any of that! How the—?' His jaw jutted at a belligerent angle and his fists clenched as if he wanted to punch someone.

'You don't think—?'

He looked at her sharply. 'That it's been sabotaged?'

'I was thinking about the windmill pump.'

'Yeah. I know. I've been thinking of that too. I'm afraid you're right. I think someone unwound the plug and left it hanging, ready to fall off.'

He turned and looked out across the empty red plain. Slowly he raised his hand to shade his eyes and did a complete three hundred and sixty degree turn, studying the wide, empty terrain carefully.

Hairs rose on the back of Charity's neck. 'What are you looking for?'

Kane's face was grim. 'If someone has deliberately crippled us,' he said, 'they could be following.'

'Watching us?' *Way out here?*

She must have sounded as frightened as she felt because he crossed the red dirt and slipped an arm around her shoulders and gave them an encouraging squeeze.

'Don't worry, Chaz. We'll be okay.' He let his arm drift back to his side and she wished he'd left it around her. She was fighting panic and she needed that reassuring hug.

'Can't we contact someone? Don't you have a radio or a phone or something?'

His mouth thinned as he grimaced. ''Fraid

not. We're out of the mobile network here and I made Reid take our satellite phone over to Lacey because he's totally on his own over there.'

No vehicle? No means of communication? She struggled to think calmly and clearly, but it was impossible. 'What can we do? We're stuck here.'

'We can walk to Tim's hideout.'

She gulped and turned to look at the distant mountains. They were still a jolly long way away. And if someone was following them... 'Will we be safe if we walk?'

'We'll stay under cover.' He gave the back of her neck a friendly rub and dropped a light kiss on the top of her head. 'We'll be okay.' He spoke gently and his smile was gentle too.

She nodded. Heavens, if Kane kept smiling at her like that she suspected she might agree to walk with him from one side of Australia to the other.

'I'm sorry about this,' he said. 'I'll never forgive myself for getting you involved. I should never have brought you to Southern Cross and I most certainly shouldn't have brought you out here.'

She managed a small smile of her own. 'I bullied you into it, remember?'

He didn't answer for a moment, just stood

there with his hand resting at her nape. 'You're a good sport, Chaz.'

Then he released her and walked to the back of the ute, and she was grateful that he didn't see her face.

Lifting the tarp covering their gear, he began to pull items out and to set them on the ground. 'We'll need hats, water and some basic food. And jackets for after sundown. And I'd better bring this,' he added, slinging a long black rifle over one shoulder.

The sight of the rifle brought another wave of panic. 'Oh, God, Kane, I hope you don't have to use that.'

'It's just a precaution,' he said and then he tossed her Annie's akubra hat and began to shove water bottles and packages of food into a backpack.

They followed a dry creek bed edged by a generous strip of shady trees, which gave them the double advantage of protective cover from possible observers as well as from the searing sun.

Kane knew that Charity was nervous about the rifle he carried and the reasons that made it necessary, so as soon as she'd safely clambered over the huge trunk of a fallen paperbark tree he tried to distract her with conversation. 'Did you tell me that you've been caring for Tim ever since he was seven?' he asked her.

'Yes,' she said. 'Since our mother died. I took over Mother's role—caring for Tim and for Father.'

'That was a tough call. You must have still been at school.'

She shrugged and swatted at a fly that dive-bombed her face. 'It wasn't easy juggling school and housework, but I missed my mother terribly and I think it was my way of coping.'

'So you've spent a long time in a household of blokes too. Like Annie.'

She smiled. 'Annie certainly has my sympathy.'

Despite the overhead shade the sun was hot on their backs as they walked. Kane kept a sharp lookout for signs of anyone following them, but he didn't want to alarm Charity so kept his vigilance as low-key as possible.

After a while she broke the silence. 'I've always thought I was like my mother—perhaps because I have her colouring.'

'That's a rather special legacy,' he said and then immediately wished he hadn't voiced his thoughts.

Luckily she acted as if she hadn't heard his

comment. Perhaps she hadn't. She seemed very intent on her explanation.

'I think that somehow I tried to—to become my mother,' she said. 'That way I could keep her alive inside me.' Shyly, she looked up at him from beneath Annie's hat. 'But that's probably more than you wanted to know.'

Thank God she had no idea how much he wanted to know about her. His head was jammed with crazy questions.

What was her favourite vegetarian food? The name of the perfume she sometimes wore? What kind of a place was Hollydean? Did she sleep easy? What did she dream about? And what the dickens was her middle name?

He cleared his throat. 'I was in my late twenties when my dad died, but it was still a really rough time.'

'Did you have to carry on his work? Running the property...'

'Yeah, but nothing felt the same any more without the old man there to give me a slap on the back.'

There was a crashing sound in the undergrowth beside them and Charity jumped. 'It's only a kangaroo,' he assured her and pointed as it loped off to their right. 'He was probably having a midday snooze and we woke him up.' After a bit he said, 'Dad's death really rocked Reid. He was even more shaken than either Annie or I. There was a point where I thought he was having some sort of breakdown, but then, after Mum went away, we had so much work on our hands we didn't have time to sit around grieving and he came good. Hard work helps, doesn't it?'

'It does.' They glanced towards each other and Kane felt his throat constrict. Her eyes were green pools inviting him to dive in.

Damn.

Soon after midday they reached a smooth shelf of granite beneath the shade of an enormous paperbark tree.

Conscious that Charity might quickly run out of energy in this heat he called a halt for lunch.

The air was very hot and still as they ate sandwiches and oranges. There was no hint of a breeze and the only sounds were the raucous cries of yellow-crested white cockatoos chasing each other overhead.

After eating only half her sandwiches Charity set them aside with a despondent little sigh, then jumped to her feet and climbed to the top of the bank to look out across the valley towards the mountains. When she returned, her expression was tense and strained and she wrapped up her food without finishing it.

'Are you ready to set off again?' Kane asked.

'No, I'm not.'

One thing about Charity, she was full of surprises.

'What's the matter? Don't you feel well?'

'I feel fine, but I'm not moving another step until you tell me exactly where Tim is and why he's there.'

'But—'

'No buts, Kane.' Her brow creased as she cast a meaningful glance over her shoulder in the direction of the hills. 'And I don't want to be diverted by any more polite conversation.'

'What's the problem?'

'I can't stand this tension. We're getting closer and closer to those ranges and, instead of feeling more relaxed, I'm getting more and more churned up. I'm worried sick. You've got to tell me what's going on, or I'll—'

Without warning, her mouth pulled out of shape and her eyes filled with tears and she dropped her face into her hands.

Kane felt lower than a snake's belly. He touched a hand to her shoulder and her head jerked up. Her green eyes were glistening and she was biting her lip to stop herself from sobbing.

'You're right,' he said. 'It's about time I filled you in.'

Hurriedly, she wiped her face with the back of her hand and sniffed loudly. 'I'm sorry. That wasn't a deliberate female ploy. It—it just happened.'

He couldn't resist a small smile. 'Deliberate or not, it works every time. Sit down a moment while I explain.'

Together they settled back on to the granite slab.

'Okay.' Charity's voice was tight with tension. 'I'm listening.'

'Well… I'm sure you've already guessed that Tim's in the ranges up there. It's a remote spot. Only our family knows about it, so he's quite safe.'

Her green gaze pierced him. 'Safe from what?'

'From trouble.'

Her eyes reflected mounting fear.

'I guess you want the whole story.'

'Of course.'

Kane sighed. 'You see, Tim was mustering out in the back country and stumbled on a massive drug crop.'

'Drugs? Good heavens. You're not growing them on Southern Cross, are you?'

'Course not. This was on a neighbouring block right near our boundary. Sometimes the cattle get through breaks in the fence line and they wander over there from time to time, so I sent Tim in to check for strays and he found a big crop of marijuana. We had to report it to the drug squad, of course, and they made some arrests.'

'Is Tim needed as a witness?'

'That's right, but drug crims are sneaky beggars, so the police want to retain him as a surprise witness.'

Charity rubbed at a streak of red dust on her jeans. 'Is that why he needed to hide?'

'Exactly.'

She thought about that for a minute, then shook her head and frowned. 'But I don't understand why he needed to hide away in these mountains. Isn't that a bit extreme?'

Kane nodded. 'Yeah, normally it would be. But Tim's situation was complicated, because a couple of the locals got to know about it and the police were worried that the big crime bosses in the city would try to silence him, or frighten him off.'

A small cry escaped her. 'But I still don't understand. If Tim's such an important witness, why didn't the police offer him some kind of protective custody?'

'They offered all right, but pigheadedness must run in your family.'

Her response was a predictable sharp-as-daggers look.

'Your brother refused police protection.'

She groaned softly. 'Silly boy.'

'Luckily, he came to his senses when someone took a pot shot at him while he was out mustering.'

'A shot?' Her face blanched. 'Oh, God, Kane.'

'He wasn't hurt,' he reassured her. 'And at least he got enough of a fright that I was able to convince him to hole up in our secret camp.'

Slumping forward with her arms wrapped around her knees, she stared at the ground. The silence of the bush floated around them while she let the news sink in.

Now be a sensible girl and let's get on with this, he wanted to add. But when she lifted her head and turned to him he saw that she was still angry.

'You could have taken me aside the day we met and told me this!'

Kane resisted the urge to call her Gingersnap again. 'Blame your brother. Tim insisted right from the start that he didn't want either you or your father to know anything.'

'But you knew we were going out of our minds with worry.'

'Yes, but Tim was worried too. He was really concerned for your safety and he was convinced that it was best if you knew nothing. He figured that the crims might be able to reach you in England if they wanted to, but they would leave you alone if it was clear that you knew nothing.'

She let out a long, shuddering sigh. 'I still think you should have told me.'

'Look, it was Tim's call. He insisted that neither the police nor my family were to tell you what had happened. Your little brother made a tough decision. That's what really troubles you, isn't it? For once in his life Tim took control without getting your permission.' When she didn't answer, he added, 'And I gave your brother my word. We shook hands.'

She frowned. 'You mean you've lied to me and kept me in emotional turmoil all because of a handshake?'

'Whoa there, Chaz. Let's get one thing straight. I didn't lie to you. I don't lie. But yes, this is all about something as small as a handshake. Out here we buy and sell properties worth millions of dollars on the shake of a hand. We commit to helping neighbours and friends with fencing and mustering. We undertake to be at a distant place at a particular time. We even make promises to English jackaroos, who show more good sense than their flaming relatives.'

One corner of her mouth tilted. 'There's no need to be so defensive, Kane. You can come down off your rock.'

Embarrassed, Kane realised he'd stepped up on to a block of granite to make his point. Jaw jutted, he rejoined her in the creek bed.

'How long is it since you've seen Tim?' she asked in a more conciliatory tone. 'Do you know if he's still safe?'

'I'm sure he's okay.'

She drew a sharp breath. 'I'm afraid I won't be happy till I see him. When's this trial?'

'Tomorrow.'

'Tomorrow? *Tomorrow?* That's crazy. How's he going to get there?'

'Our plan was that I would pick him up today and take him straight through to Mirrabrook. In the ute.' He offered a small, self-deprecating smile. 'But now—with Reid gone and Vic injured and with the engine damaged—I'm not much use to him.'

'So Tim won't be able to give evidence after all?'

'He has a horse. I'm afraid he's going to have to use it. But he'll have to set out this afternoon if he's going to make it in time.'

She groaned.

'It'll still work out, Charity.'

Leaping to her feet, she cried, 'What on earth are we doing, sitting here as if we're on a picnic? Come on, Kane. Let's get going.'

Without waiting, she began to charge off at twice their previous pace. Grabbing the backpack and rifle, Kane followed.

Their boots crunched loudly as they stomped over the gravel bed of the creek. 'Hey,' Kane shouted. 'You won't last the distance if you don't take this a little easier.'

He was wrong.

To his amazement she kept up the same fierce pace for the next two hours, not even pausing for drink stops, but taking sips from her water bottle as she went.

It wasn't easy walking. The creek bed was littered with rocks, large and small, but Charity had the fierce, unflagging energy of a lioness in search of a lost cub.

Pearls of perspiration glistened on her skin. Beneath her shady hat, her hair lay in damp, coppery coils against her face, and her heavy braid made a V-shaped patch on the back of her shirt between her shoulder blades. But still she pressed on.

'I believe you now, when you said you climbed Mount Snowdon,' Kane told her.

'You mean you didn't believe me before?'

'Well—you don't look like a mountain climber. You have such a delicate air.'

'Oh, nonsense.' Despite her anxiety, she wrinkled her nose and sent him an impudent smile. 'My colouring might suggest that I'm delicate, but don't let that deceive you. The rest of me is quite—'

She didn't finish the sentence. Instead, her smile vanished and she pulled her hat even lower over her face and almost ran ahead as if she needed to put some distance between them.

Kane watched her confusion with wry amusement. No doubt she was embarrassed by her admission. She'd be even more embarrassed if she knew how many ways he'd already devised to test her claim.

Testing Charity Denham for delicacy... It was a version of the fantasy that had plagued him for days now.

He would start by testing her delicate mouth...taking his time over long, slow, exquisitely delicate kisses. And then he would need to assess the delicacy of her breasts, to discover whether they were tipped by the same delicate pink as her lips.

And then there was the rest of her...

Oh, hell. What was the point in torturing himself? There were a thousand reasons why he should never be privy to any of Charity Denham's delicate charms.

Matching his pace to hers, he said gruffly, 'I hope those boots of Annie's fit you well. If you get blisters you'll know all about delicate feet.'

She ignored him.

Sensible girl.

Around mid-afternoon they left the dry creek bed and crossed a short stretch of open plain to the foot of the mountain range. Here a flowing creek emerged after tumbling from the top of the range in a series of waterfalls and cascades.

'Not long to go now, but the last part is uphill,' he warned her.

With one hand holding her hat in place, she stood with her head tilted back, looking up. 'How far do we have to climb?'

Before he could answer, a loud 'Cooee!' rang down the mountainside.

She gave an excited little jump and grabbed Kane's arm. 'Did you hear that? It's Tim, isn't it?'

'Sounds like him.' He grinned. 'He still hasn't quite mastered the bush call—but he's getting better.' Narrowing his eyes, he searched for signs of movement in the foliage and rocks above them. 'I'd say he's seen us and is on his way down.'

'Oh, thank heavens.' Her eyes shone as she hurried forward. 'Come on, let's go.'

'Hang on, Chaz. Follow me, or you'll get lost.'

But his warning was unnecessary. Before they'd properly begun their ascent, Tim Denham appeared suddenly, striding out of the thick scrub.

Charity gave a shriek and lunged forward.

The young man's mouth sagged open as he recognised his sister beneath the akubra. 'Charity,' he cried. 'What the hell are you doing here?'

Not bothering to answer, she hurled herself at him and threw her arms around him.

Tim directed a glare over her head at Kane. 'What's going on, Kane? You promised to keep my family out of this.'

'Hush, Tim. Don't blame Kane. I didn't give him much choice. Aren't you pleased to see me?'

'Well…yes…of course.'

CHAPTER SEVEN

THE reunion, Charity decided later, was something of an anticlimax. After the first wonderful surge of happy relief, she'd had to make some quick mental adjustments. She'd been so worried about her brother. So full of fear. So haunted by her ghastly dreams. And in her most anxious moments she'd tended to think of Tim as a little boy still—lost and in trouble and in need of her.

But here he was—looking fantastic—so handsome and adventurous in his dark blue shirt and jeans and broad-brimmed akubra hat. The same old Tim, but somehow taller, stronger, fitter. So very grown up.

Dark stubble lined his jaw and his black hair was long enough to curl at his collar. And, dear heaven, there was a rifle slung over his shoulder.

'I still can't believe it's you, Charity,' he said, once Kane had explained everything and he'd calmed down. 'I thought it was Annie who'd come with Kane.'

'I had to come. I—I've been so worried.'

Tim was happy to see her of course. He hugged her fiercely and let her hug him, but she was careful not to overwhelm him with sentimentality. And she knew she mustn't, *mustn't* cry.

'I'm really sorry I couldn't let you know where I was,' he said. 'I know I promised Father I'd stay in touch, and I knew you both would be worried…but I never dreamed you'd come all this way to look for me.' He turned to Kane. 'How much have you told her?'

'I've had to fill her in, mate. Whoever tampered with the ute has also been snooping around Southern Cross, frightening the daylights out of Charity.'

Tim let out a horrified moan.

'And poor old Vic copped a broken arm after someone sabotaged the windmill.'

After that the two men huddled to discuss what Tim must do next.

As they talked, Charity feasted her eyes on her brother. There was something significantly different about him and it involved more than the physical changes she'd noticed immediately.

Instead of being cowed by his situation, she sensed an air of confidence, as if Tim had acquired an inner strength. Was that what came from living it tough on the land? From living with danger and coming to terms with it? From working with the McKinnon men?

All these weeks she'd been picturing him as lost and frightened, but when she looked at him now she knew he was managing just fine on his own. She tried not to mind that her role as his caregiver was well and truly over.

Their time together was disappointingly brief.

Tim took them to a large overhanging ledge on a beautiful ridge and Charity was pleasantly surprised to see that the mountain cave where he'd camped wasn't dark and forbidding, but airy and full of light. Tim proudly offered her and Kane damper that he'd baked over the coals, and they spread it with honey he'd gathered from wild beehives in the bush. But their meal was rushed and in no time he was making preparations to hurry on horseback back to Southern Cross.

'Ride to the ringers' shack and get Ferret to take you to Senior Sergeant Jackson in Mirrabrook,' Kane told Tim. 'And then the police will get you to Townsville for the trial. You should get out of the rough country while you still have daylight.

'There'll be a full moon, so you'll have plenty of light to guide you for most of the ride. Don't take the boundary track. Use the route via the number seventeen bore. That will cut you through the back way. And tell Ferret to bring a vehicle out to collect us tomorrow.'

Charity had been busy admiring how easily Tim understood these strange directions and it took a few moments for this last instruction to sink in. *Tomorrow?* She turned to Kane in dismay. 'Do you mean we're going to have to stay here tonight?'

There was a flash of silver-blue as his eyes widened momentarily and then he smiled and sent her a slow, teasing wink. 'Don't worry, Chaz. You'll make a great cavewoman.'

Electricity slid down her spine. Until that moment she hadn't given a thought to anything beyond her brother's safety. But suddenly she was thinking about herself. And the night ahead. In vivid, body-melting detail.

She and Kane would have to stay here. They had no transport, so they had no choice. They would have to sleep on the bedding that Tim had spread on the sandy floor of the cave. Just the two of them.

Too late, she realised that Tim was watching them both closely. His intelligent gaze shot from Kane's winking smile to her hot face and back to Kane again, and his eyes narrowed shrewdly. He opened his mouth as if he planned to ask a question, but then he stopped as if he needed to think more carefully before he spoke.

She gulped. *Oh, man.* Was her little brother concerned about leaving her with Kane? Was he worried about her virtue?

Tim's hazel eyes were studying her thoughtfully and she held her breath for fear she might do something foolish—like blush.

She wanted to tell him that if he imagined there was anything *going on* between herself and Kane he was one hundred and ten per cent wrong. But it would sound ridiculous if she tried to tell her little brother that. Impossible with Kane standing there watching them.

Then Tim said, 'I'm sorry to have to desert you so soon, Charity, but at least I know you're in good hands with Kane.' An ambiguous smile tilted his mouth. 'The man's a legend.'

Behind them, Kane cleared his throat.

'Don't worry about your sister,' he said. 'She might have arrived here only a few days ago, but already she's had to deal with a rash of new experiences and she's risen to every challenge like a trooper.'

'Of course she has,' Tim said, his eyes blazing with a flash of fierce, brotherly pride. 'My sister is as plucky as they come.'

The two men stood to attention, gazes locked, and for five pulsing seconds an unspoken message passed between them.

Charity couldn't bear this silly tension. 'Don't even think about me. You take care,' she said to Tim and she hugged him hard. 'Make sure you ring Father as soon as you're anywhere near a telephone.'

'Yes, I promise. Now, stop worrying, sis.' He kissed her cheek and gave her one last hug, suddenly squeezing her tight the way he used to when he was little and needed her.

'I won't be happy until this whole trial is over and you're free to get on with your life,' she told him.

'*Don't worry.* I'm having the *time* of my life.'

She waited at the wide mouth of the cave while Kane accompanied Tim down the track to the base of the ridge where the horse was tethered. She felt strangely deflated.

This was it. She'd achieved her goal. Her crusade was complete. She'd found Tim. And the irony was that he hadn't even wanted to be found.

The loving big sister—who'd rushed bravely to the wild Antipodes, ready to hack her way through red tape, through jungles, and past secretive outback cattlemen, or whatever it took—had to face the fact that her grand gesture was a fizzer. She wasn't needed.

And all she had to do now was to spend a night alone in a cave in the wilderness with a man she'd been lusting after from the moment she'd set eyes on him.

If Marsha knew she and Kane were alone out here she'd be emerald with envy. But what a joke. As if Charity Denham, the goody-goody daughter of the rector of St Alban's, Hollydean, was going to spend a night of blazing passion with one of the sexiest men in the known universe.

Get real, girl.

Out of nowhere, tears that she'd held at bay while Tim was watching spilled down her cheeks. She told herself it was an understandable reaction to being parted from her brother so soon after finding him. She'd been so sure her world would be right when she found Tim.

But it didn't feel right at all.

Just the same it was ridiculous to cry. The last thing she wanted was for Kane to come back and find her in tears.

Swiping at her damp face with her shirt sleeve, she drew in a long, deep, steadying breath. She was tired from the long hike in the heat and her feet were stinging and she suspected she had blisters, so she pulled off her boots and examined the damage. They weren't too bad—a couple of small blisters on her heels.

There was a rock pool at the mouth of the cave. She sat on a sun-warmed rock at the edge of the pool and dangled her feet in the cool water, looking around her and taking careful stock of her surroundings.

Actually, Tim's cave looked surprisingly comfortable. No doubt estate agents from the caveman era would have been pretty excited about its attractions: the pretty terracotta walls; the high cathedral ceilings and soft white sandy floor; the fern-fringed rock pool right at the front door and the spectacular view clear across the Star Valley. Position, position, position!

And inside the cave there was a large metal trunk filled with provisions—tinned and dried food, eating utensils and cooking gear and a stone-lined fireplace. It was obvious that Tim had been well provided for.

Resting back on her elbows, she tilted her head and looked up at the vivid blue sky stretching wide and high overhead. The world was so still and quiet here. Apart from the toots and chirrups of birds, there was an almost spiritual silence.

The appeal of the outback crept up on you,

she decided. There was so much more to it
than first met the eye. It wasn't just heat and
dust and gum trees.

She was used to the obvious prettiness of
her homeland—the softer landscape of the
woods and the fells, the quaint winding country lanes and charming villages. The outback,
on the other hand, tended to guard its beauty
like a well kept secret. But when you un-
earthed the glamour—like this rock pool sus-
pended high above the valley—the effect was
breathtaking.

If only she had her art equipment. How
wonderful it would be to paint this scene. She
would capture it all—this pool of glass-green
water fringed by rocks and ferns, the aston-
ishing blue of the sky and the pretty pattern
of shadows cast by clouds drifting across the
valley.

In the foreground she would highlight the
brilliant crimson of the bottle brush flowers on
the small shrubs growing out of crevices in
the rocks, and the dramatic contrast of the
black and white butterflies that fluttered
around them.

'That's a pensive face.'

Startled, she spun around to see Kane
crossing the rocks towards her.

'I didn't hear you. Has Tim gone?'

'Yes.'

'Will he be okay?'

'Sure. If you watch closely you might see the dust from his horse's hooves.'

She peered back down into the valley.

'There,' he said, pointing, and goose bumps broke out on her arms as he squatted beside her.

She caught sight of a faint white cloud trailing through the scrub.

They watched the dust trail for ages until eventually it disappeared amidst the distant trees.

'Great view, isn't it?' said Kane.

'Marvellous. I wish I'd brought a camera with me. I'd love to take some of these memories home.'

He didn't reply for a moment, then he said, 'When we get back to Southern Cross you should take a squiz at some of my photographs. I have quite a few shots taken from here and you're welcome to help yourself.'

'Thanks. I'd really love that.' She smiled, but the smile didn't stick very well because the thought of going home created an inexplicable hollowness in her chest. But of course she should leave soon. If Tim was fine she really didn't have any excuse to hang around. It wasn't as if the housekeeping she'd done at

Southern Cross was indispensable. And her father needed her back at St Alban's.

Hunting for a change of subject, she asked, 'What does it feel like to look out there and know that you own all that land?'

Kane seemed to give her question some thought and settled himself more comfortably on to the rock before he spoke. 'It's not a feeling of ownership so much. It's more a sense of belonging to the land and a kind of gratitude for having the chance to live in this country and work with it.'

'You love it, don't you?'

'Absolutely.' He smiled. 'Maybe it's my Scottish blood. They reckon it was mainly the Scots who pushed beyond their comfort zone and settled in Australia's toughest marginal country.'

'Well, my family has been English as far back as we can trace, but I've been thinking how much I'd love to paint this.'

'Really? Are you an artist?'

'No, I can't claim to be an artist. I'd like to be one, but—' She shrugged. 'This sounds like the lamest excuse under the sun, but I never seem to have time.'

'I guess you're too busy being a Sunday school teacher and chief cook and bottle-washer.'

'Something like that.'

'Pity,' he said softly. 'You deserve some free time to do things for yourself.'

He sounded so understanding that she felt emboldened to add, 'When I was at school, my art teachers were very encouraging. I'll get back to painting one day.'

'After you find a rich husband.'

She nearly pitched forward into the pool. The word husband coming out of Kane's mouth sent hot and cold flashes chasing up and down and through her. How silly. *She had to get a grip.* 'A rich husband,' she repeated as coolly as she could manage. 'Now that's an idea. I wish I'd thought of that strategy before now. You're so right. I need a lovely man who'll indulge my whims and let me paint to my heart's content.'

'I thought every woman was on the lookout for an indulgent husband.'

Charity didn't dare look at him, but his voice hummed with familiar teasing amusement. She forced a smile. 'I've got my priorities wrong, haven't I? I should have been hunting for a husband, not a lost little brother. Especially as my brother didn't consider himself lost.'

'That's right,' he said. 'Just remember when you go home that you need to keep a weather eye open for an utterly cultured British chap with pots of money. Someone who'll set you up with a nice little London flat and a house in the country.'

'*And* a house in the country?' she repeated with forced brightness. 'Somehow that sounds more like a mistress than a wife.'

'Well... I suppose being his mistress could be another option.'

Something in his voice compelled her to look up. His eyes met hers. *Oh, help!* She felt as if he were burning her with his gaze.

But then, quite suddenly, the fire left his eyes and he shook his head slowly. Finally, he smiled. 'Perhaps not. You're not the mistress type, are you, Chaz?'

Abruptly, she lifted her feet out of the water, making a loud swoosh and she dripped water across the shelf of rock as she swung her legs sideways before tucking them neatly beside her.

'This is the most ridiculous conversation I've ever had.' Her voice sounded too tight, too high. 'It all started because I said I wanted to paint this lovely rock pool and the view. I certainly won't be able to paint it if I'm gadding about England being a kept woman, shunting backwards and forwards between a flat in Notting Hill and my lover's house in the country.'

Kane didn't answer for the longest time. A flight of birds swept overhead and a cloud drifted across the valley. The sun dipped a notch closer to the western horizon.

'Well...' he said eventually. 'If you really want to paint this scenery, you'd be welcome back here any time.'

It was the kind of polite invitation he might offer to anyone and she wished with all her heart that it didn't make her feel so sad.

CHAPTER EIGHT

THE dark shadows on the cave walls were broken by flickering orange firelight.

Kane leaned over her. 'Have you ever been kissed in a cave, Chaz?'

She lay on a swag on the cave floor and her body thrummed with wanting him.

'No,' she whispered. 'What about you? Have you been kissed in a cave?'

'Can't say I have.'

He smiled and it was such a beautiful smile she needed to make it hers, to touch it with her lips, to taste it with her tongue.

'Don't you agree that I need to expand my repertoire of new experiences?' she said in an unfamiliar coquettish purr. 'A kiss in a cave would be a good starting point.'

His eyes smouldered with unmistakable desire. 'My thoughts exactly.'

Then he leaned closer and his shoulders blocked the fire's light, so she lay in darkness, quivering with exquisite anticipation. Her moist, eager lips parted to greet him.

And Kane's mouth lowered gently over hers.

His kiss was hot, powerful, passionate. Perfect.

Magic. One touch of his lips and she became the sexiest woman in the world. Tilting her head back, she arched wantonly, lifting her urgent body towards him, offering everything, and...

She woke.

She woke to discover that she was cold.

The fire had burned low and was no more than a small heap of red coals. Pulling her jacket closer around her, she saw moonlight flooding the cave, coating everything with cool silver. She felt suddenly bereft, in mourning for the intoxicating excitement of her dream.

Then she saw that the swag beside her was empty and her heart thumped painfully as she bolted into a sitting position. Where was Kane?

Leaning sideways, she felt his bedding. No warmth at all. What had happened to him? She'd been so exhausted; she must have fallen asleep almost as soon as she'd finished her dinner. She couldn't even remember whether Kane had come to bed.

Scrambling to her feet, she called his

name—calling softly because she was frightened. There was no answer but out of the corner of her eye she caught a slight movement near the mouth of the cave.

Panic leapt in her stomach as she saw a tall, dark inhuman shape. Her mouth shot open, ready to scream. But then her eyes adjusted to the light and the shape morphed into Kane— Kane settling his back more comfortably against a tall boulder as he stared out into the night.

For heaven's sake. Hauling her jacket more tightly around her, she hurried over the sandy floor in her bare feet. 'Kane?'

He swung around. 'What are you doing up?'

'I woke because I was cold. But what about you? Why aren't you sleeping?'

'I wanted to keep watch.'

'Watch? Have you been standing out here all night?'

He didn't answer.

In the silvery moonlight his face looked as if it had been carved from rock. It was as remote as the moon.

'Go back to sleep,' he said.

She couldn't. Not when she knew he was out here standing sentry. Keeping watch to protect her. All night. Surely after the long hike he must have been as tired as she was?

With her arms wrapped around her for warmth, she took a couple of steps forward out of the cave and looked up into the night sky. 'Oh, my,' she said. 'Now I know why they call this place the Star Valley.'

The sky was ablaze. There were so many stars she felt dizzy. 'I've never seen anything like it,' she said. 'The stars are so *bright* here. And there are so many.'

She looked around her at the rocks and trees and then out across the valley. The outback at night was as vast and silent as an empty cathedral. And as splendid. The entire side of the mountain was dipped in silver. 'Oh, look,' she cried. 'The moon's reflected in the rock pool. Isn't it beautiful?'

Kane didn't answer, but when she turned back to him she saw that he was watching her. And, despite the soft silvery focus of the moonlight, his eyes seemed to burn. She could feel the force of his gaze scorching deep inside her, touching her intimately.

She remembered her dream and a starburst of liquid longing swept through her. She couldn't breathe. *Touch me, Kane. Kiss me. Please.*

'Do—do you know what the t-time is?' she asked.

'About four. Plenty of time for you to go back to bed and get some more sleep.'

But how could she possibly sleep? If she lay down again, all she would do was think about him. She had to talk. Talking was safe. Far safer than brooding, burning silence.

'Do you know where Tim might be by now?'

'He rides well and he's on a good horse, so I'd say he'd have reached Ferret by now. They could be on the way into Mirrabrook already.'

She sighed. 'I'm not sleepy any more. I'll stay and keep you company for a bit.' She found a smooth, flat boulder that made a comfortable seat. 'I'm never going to see stars like this after I go home, so I want to drink my fill.'

Propping her feet on the edge of the rock, she drew her knees in close, so that she could wrap her arms around them. 'Just imagine, Kane, thousands of years ago, Aborigines probably lived in this cave and looked out at these very same stars.'

She heard his soft chuckle. 'You *are* in a talkative mood, aren't you?'

My alternative is to kiss you, Kane, but I'm way too chicken to try that.

She sat very still, staring out into the night, trying not to think about her dream and how much she wanted this man to hold her, to make love to her.

'Actually, the Aborigines have a legend about how the stars were made,' he said.

'Do you know it?'

'More or less. They claim that an old man captured two beautiful women, but one of them escaped into a swamp. So he chased her with a burning fire stick in his hand. As soon as the fire stick touched the water, the sparks hissed and scattered to the sky and became golden stars.'

'That's so clever,' she cried. 'The stars look exactly like sparks from a fire stick.' Sitting with her chin resting on her knees, she stared out at the jet-black sky, speckled with a trillion fiery specks. 'What happened to the woman? Did he catch her?'

'No, she dived beneath the swamp waters and got away.'

'And the other one? The one who didn't escape?'

'The old man kept her and turned her into the evening star.'

She smiled. 'I suppose there could be worse fates.'

An awkward silence fell over them and she

found her thoughts dwelling on what usually happened to a woman when a man chased her and caught her. Annoyed to find herself thinking about *that* again, she jumped to her feet and from somewhere up the mountain came a spine-chilling hissing sound. 'What's that?' she cried, scampering closer to Kane.

An eerie whistle ricocheted past them, then continued on down into the valley.

'It's only an owl.'

'An owl? But it sounded like a bomb. You know—like the old-fashioned ones in the World War Two movies?'

He smiled. 'No, Chaz. It was definitely just an owl.'

His smile sent high octane excitement shivering through her. Oh, help. Why was she so susceptible to this man? Was it simply because he was so big and strong and protective? So male and...

'How on earth can you stay awake all night?' she asked him. 'You must be exhausted. It can't be necessary, Kane. Tim slept here without a guard.'

He shrugged. 'This isn't the first time I've stayed awake all night. Don't worry. I'm fine.'

'Do you think someone might have followed us here?'

'It's possible. I'm not prepared to take risks.'

'It's very chivalrous of you.'

'There's nothing chivalrous about it, Chaz. It's simply common sense.'

But she'd had a lifetime of common sense and she wanted to cast it to the winds. The impulse to step close and to kiss his cheek was so strong that she acted on it without waiting for second thoughts. But, before her lips could touch his beard-rough skin, Kane stiffened.

'Don't,' he growled and she jumped back as if he'd slapped her.

'I only wanted to thank you.'

'Just get back to bed, Charity.'

'There's no need to bite my head off.'

'You should know better than to throw yourself at a man when you're alone with him in the middle of the night.' His voice was deep, rasping and thickened by anger.

'Throw myself? Why would I want to throw myself at *you?*' She was hurt and embarrassed and ten times angrier than he was. 'All I was planning was one harmless thank you kiss on the cheek. But, don't worry, I won't waste the effort.'

She was about to spin away from him when, without warning, his hand whipped out of the darkness to cup her chin.

She gasped.

Kane held her with her mouth trapped breathless inches from his and she knew she should pull away. She should object. She should tell him he had no right to manhandle her. But, mercy…how could she protest when every quivering instinct told her that Kane was about to kiss her?

She could sense his tension, hear the violent rasp of his breathing. Was he experiencing the same havoc, the same untamed longing that stormed her body? Already she was losing any sense of control; she was a wilting flower held too close to his flame.

Her eyes drifted closed, her lips open. She trembled.

Yes, kiss me, Kane. Now. Please.

'Chaz!' His voice grated with impatience and she felt his hand release her.

Her eyes shot open.

'If you know what's good for you, you'll get going now.'

'G-going?'

'Get back into that cave and stay there.'

Shocked and feeling like a foolish, love-struck schoolgirl, she hurried back into the cave—almost scampering like a whipped puppy. She buried herself deep inside the swag and wished that she could vanish. Right now, the thought of being turned into a star and banished to a far-flung corner of the universe sounded much more appealing than being stuck in the bush with Kane McKinnon.

Only one little kiss...

Kane suppressed a groan. Hadn't Charity known he was going out of his mind with wanting her? Couldn't she guess that she'd been driving him wild for days now?

All night he'd been out here, trying not to think about her warm sweet body lying mere metres away. Trying not to think about threading his fingers through the fiery silk of her hair. Trying not to imagine the taste of her tempting pink mouth, or how her soft, round breasts would fit perfectly in his palms. Trying not to dwell on countless variations of his theory for testing her delicacy.

One kiss—even a kiss on the cheek—would be one kiss too many. One tiny kiss and his control would shatter. In a flash he'd be down on that bedding with her and her virtue would be a thing of the past.

And wouldn't that be a smart move? The big bad cattleman had his wicked way with the Sunday school teacher. The ultimate cliché.

The ultimate flaming catastrophe.

What kind of man took advantage of a vicar's daughter entrusted into his care by her brother?

Even now when he was blameless, it would be bad enough. When he got back to Southern Cross, speculation would be rife. Reid, Ferret...old Vic...Tim...all of them would have their beady eyes pinned on himself and Charity.

Those blokes would be like hawks waiting to pounce...sniffing for evidence...trying to second guess what had happened during his night alone with this lovely girl.

As he glared out into the bush, a scrub turkey came scratching around, searching for food, and he shooed it away with an angry flick of his hand.

The heck of it was that Charity Denham wasn't a girl he'd want for a one-night stand. If the timing and the circumstances had allowed, he might have wooed her properly with dates and dinners and dancing and all the things a girl liked.

But the timing was crap. And the circumstances were worse. And what was the point? Her business in Australia was finished and she had no plans to stay. Why would she want to stay in the dangerous and remote outback when she had a safe haven in England?

She would be as keen as his own mother to shake the outback dust from her heels.

Dawn trudged around at last. They made billy tea for breakfast and poked thin green sticks through slices of bread and held them out over the coals till they turned into crisp, smoky toast, which tasted surprisingly good smeared with Tim's bush honey. But their meal took up too little time.

They spent a difficult day hanging around the cave waiting for Ferret. It was terribly hot and they swam in the rock pool. Kane stripped down to boxer shorts, brief enough to send Charity's temperature soaring. Although she removed her jeans, she kept her shirt on and its long tails covered her discreetly. Afterwards, she sat on a rock to drip dry.

She and Kane were excessively self-conscious, so they talked about Tim and the trial, about Reid and the Lacey Downs stockman's little premature baby, about Annie, about Charity's father...about everybody and anybody they could think of...except themselves.

It was as if they were frightened to find out too much about each other. And Charity wondered if it was because they were frightened that they might like what they discovered.

Kane didn't even comment on the colour of her hair when it was wet.

He had been right to reject her last night. She'd been fooling herself that it was only a friendly peck on the cheek that she'd planned. They both knew better than that. But what was the point of getting emotionally involved? It would be silly to get all churned up about Kane when she was about to go home. Hemispheres away.

They were both hugely relieved when Ferret arrived shortly after lunch.

To Charity's surprise, Kane insisted on driving and Ferret seemed quite happy to give up control of his vehicle.

'You'll be more comfortable at the window,' Kane told her. 'And Ferret can sit in the middle.'

Once the three of them were inside the cramped cabin she realised that Kane was making sure that he didn't have to spend the journey with her body anywhere near his as they rode over the bumpy track. Ferret, on the other hand, seemed to find the arrangement just fine. He sat in the middle with his thigh pressed hard against hers, and he grinned for most of the way home.

Luckily he wasn't big on conversation and his ute didn't have air-conditioning, so they drove with the windows down, which made conversation almost impossible. That suited Charity. All she wanted now was to get back to Southern Cross, to have a shower and shampoo her hair and to telephone her father to discuss plans for going home.

At sundown, Kane strolled into the kitchen to fetch a cold beer from the fridge and realised too late that Charity was still on the telephone talking to her father in England.

'So I should be able to fly home as soon as the trial's over,' she was saying.

Not wanting to eavesdrop, he turned on his heel and was about to leave again, when her voice rose on a sharp note of panic. 'Why?' she cried. 'But you need me, don't you?'

She was standing with her back to Kane, so he could see the way her shoulders hunched with tension and she was clutching the receiver so tightly her knuckles were white. Her other hand was pressed into the centre of her chest, as if she were trying to block a sudden pain.

Had her father told her bad news? Kane took a step closer, wondering if she needed help.

'Alice?' she shouted into the phone. 'Alice

Bainbridge?' Her voice was thin and sharp. Shocked. 'Is she? Oh—I—I see.'

She slumped on to a kitchen stool, her attention riveted to the speaker at the other end of the line.

'Really?' She made a choked, gasping sound. 'Well, of course I'm surprised, but it's—it's lovely news.'

Kane knew he should leave but he was transfixed by the stricken note in Charity's voice. Why was she so distressed by news she proclaimed to be lovely?

'I—I'm so happy for you,' she said in what sounded dangerously close to a sob. 'No, no I'm not crying. I'm fine, Father... Yes, of course, I'm thrilled for you... All right, I'll give it some thought and get back to you. Bye, darling. Give my—give my love to—Alice.'

The minute she hung up the phone, she collapsed into a huddle on the stool.

'Charity,' Kane said. 'What is it? Have you had bad news?'

She didn't seem to hear him at first and he touched her on the shoulder. 'Chaz?'

Her head jerked up and she stared at him with stunned, huge eyes that welled with shiny tears.

'What is it? Have you had bad news?' he asked again.

'No,' she sobbed, but her chin quivered and her mouth pulled out of shape and he knew she was terribly upset.

Unsure what to say next, he waited for her explanation. When it didn't come, he asked, 'You're not all right, are you?'

'No.' She squeezed her eyes shut and pressed a hand over her mouth as if she were trying to gather control. It didn't seem to work. A sob burst from her lips and she jumped from the stool and dashed out of the kitchen.

Kane felt compelled to follow.

She headed for the back veranda, and stood at the railing, staring out across the home paddock, which was awash with the purple shadows of twilight. He could see at a glance that her shoulders were shaking.

Feeling helpless, he almost turned and went back into the house. A woman's tears were *so* not his scene. But this was Chaz and she was in trouble and somehow he felt responsible for her.

He stepped up beside her. 'Anything I can do to help?'

'No, Kane.' Still staring out across the paddock, she drew a long, deep breath and then released it. 'I'm actually being very, very silly. I'll be absolutely fine in a moment.'

'You want me to hang around?'

'No,' she said. Then suddenly, 'I mean yes. Yes, please.' She turned slowly to face him and leant her hips back against the railing.

He could see that she tried to smile but it didn't work, so she took another breath.

'My father's getting married again,' she said. 'So you see, I have absolutely no right to be upset.'

'But you are.'

She nodded and gave a self-deprecating roll of her eyes. 'I have no idea why.'

'I take it this news has come as a surprise?'

'Absolutely.' Lifting her hands in a gesture of helplessness, she gave a shaky little laugh. 'He's marrying Alice Bainbridge—one of the Mothers' Union ladies. The irony is that I organised for her to look after him while I was away.'

He cracked a grin. 'She must have done an excellent job.'

'I'll say.' She frowned. 'Now that I think back, I'm pretty sure she volunteered. With great enthusiasm.'

'Sounds like your dad was a marked man.'

'Probably.'

'Don't you approve of her?'

'Oh, what's not to approve about Alice? She's perfect for him—quite lovely, really.

She's a widow with two grown-up children—an attractive, wealthy widow, and a good parish worker who attends church every Sunday.'

She screwed her eyes tightly shut as if she needed to suppress a fresh flood of tears.

'It's the kind of news that takes a little getting used to,' he suggested.

Her eyes opened again as she nodded. 'Honestly, I'm not upset because my father's getting married.'

'So there's something else bothering you?'

She shook her head. 'Don't worry, Kane. Thanks for your concern, but you wouldn't understand.'

'Try me.'

Their eyes met and a jolt of unexpected emotion caused a logjam in Kane's throat. Damn, but her eyes were a beautiful green and, when they were made starry by tears and rimmed by damp, dark lashes, they were more lovely than ever. If he wasn't very careful he was going to get lost in those eyes one day very soon, and there was every chance he'd never find his way out.

'It's crazy,' she said, 'but I'm feeling a total mess because everyone else is so happy. Tim's happy and Father's happy and—' Her mouth trembled and she shot him a look of wretched confusion. 'They don't need me any more,' she said, and then suddenly her face seemed to collapse, and she was crying as if her heart would break.

There was no way Kane could resist hauling her into his arms and cradling her head against his shoulder.

Her body felt so slender as she trembled against him. Her skin smelled of soap from her recent shower and her hair of shampoo.

Feeling several versions of helpless, he made soothing noises as he stroked her hair and her head, her neck. She snuggled close and his body responded with such alacrity he almost gave in to the moment.

Remember this is Charity. Don't do anything crazy, man. Don't try to kiss her. Don't think about how good she smells, how damn sexy she feels.

Drawing on reserves of control he didn't know he had, he managed to hold her without losing his mind. But as soon as she began to calm down he took her by the shoulders and eased her gently away from him.

'I'm sorry, Kane,' she said as she dragged her sleeve over her eyes. 'I'm going to pull myself together any minute now.'

'How about a cup of tea?' he suggested,

grabbing at the remedy most outback women turned to when they were feeling low.

'Yes, thanks. That would be good. I'll go and wash my face.'

When Charity came back into the kitchen she felt more composed, although the bathroom mirror had shown her that she still looked pale and watery-eyed—which was exactly how she didn't want to look in front of Kane.

They sat at the kitchen table with the big brown teapot and two mugs between them.

She watched his strong, work-toughened hand gripping the teapot's handle as he poured the tea into their mugs and marvelled at how gently he'd held her just a few minutes ago.

'I'm terribly sorry that I blubbered all over you like that,' she said as she lifted her mug. 'I don't know why I lost it.'

'It's not so surprising.' He concentrated on stirring two spoonfuls of sugar into his tea. 'You've been looking after your father and Tim for a long time. Caring for them was your job for years and years—and now you suddenly find that Tim's taking care of himself and your father's found a wife, which makes you feel redundant. You've copped a pretty hefty blow.'

'I guess my ego must be more fragile than I'd realised.'

'I'm no psychologist, Chaz, but you said that you threw yourself into the role of family carer as a way of getting over your mother's death. And now that caring role has been taken away suddenly, so a huge gap has opened up in your life. You'll need a little time to adjust.'

'Yes,' she whispered.

They sipped tea in silence for a minute or two.

'What you need to come to terms with now is the fact that you're free to think of yourself for a change.'

'Yes, I guess so.'

'You can take up painting, or whatever takes your fancy.'

'Yes.' Right now she couldn't get excited about any of that.

He cleared his throat. 'Reid rang while you were in the bathroom.'

'Has he been able to get through to Annie?'

'Yes, thank God.'

'How is she?'

'She's okay. Apparently, she was still a little vague about what she's actually doing in Brisbane, but she's convinced Reid that she's fine.' Kane fiddled with the handle of his mug. 'Reid found us a cook, too.'

'A cook?'

'Yeah. Reid's decided that we've taken Annie too much for granted.'

'Have you?'

He grinned sheepishly. 'Probably. She deserves a chance to test her wings for a bit in the big smoke, so Reid's found some bloke in Hughenden who's been a cook on mustering teams and in station homesteads for thirty years or more. He's something of a bush legend and Reid's offered him a job here.'

'I see.'

'What's the matter? I thought you'd be pleased.'

'Why?'

'For all the reasons we've just been talking about. You're free. You don't have to hang around here any more. You can leave Star Valley. The world, as they say, is your oyster.'

Staring at a crack in the scrubbed pine surface of the ancient kitchen table, she knew that it was all very well for Kane to offer her helpful suggestions, but there was one problem with his advice. One big, fat, hopelessly unsolvable problem.

She didn't want the world. And the oyster she wanted above all others was sitting across the table from her—the man who'd held her as if she were a highly treasured possession. The one with eyes like the morning sky, who could melt her bones with a single glance.

But she would never be able to tell him that, because he wasn't on offer, so instead she said, 'Whenever it's convenient for you to take me into town, I'll be on my way.'

It was exactly the opposite of what she wanted, but thank heavens she'd kept her voice under control so he would never guess.

A dark shadow flickered in the depths of his eyes and his face stiffened. He twisted the mug between his hands and for longer than Charity could bear he didn't answer. But then he spoke without looking at her.

'I have to collect Vic some time in the next few days, so I should be able to give you a lift then.'

CHAPTER NINE

KANE knew that he couldn't keep Charity on Southern Cross, but over the next two days he made no attempt to help her to leave.

He wasn't prepared to analyse why. He just let things drift, knowing that any day soon, someone—Reid, Vic or Annie—would return and then he would have to let Charity go. In the meantime he skirted around the question of her going. God knew why. Having her here, under his roof, was torture.

He spent two days in bittersweet torment. He tried to stay away from her—working outside as much as possible. In the evenings he closeted himself in the study pretending to do paperwork. But there were the mealtimes to be shared...and all the countless other times he found excuses to seek her out...

He kept needing to see her, to feast his eyes on her, to watch her beautiful hands doing everyday things like setting the table...to listen to her voice, to catch her smile...

He'd never put himself through this kind of

self-imposed agony before. In the past, if he'd wanted a woman, he'd done something about it.

But this woman was different. If he started something with her, he would want it to go on for ever. And that wasn't going to happen. She would want to escape.

He found himself thinking of ridiculous comparisons, like the time when he was six years old and he'd tried to keep a butterfly in a jar. It had died, of course. And then, at ten, he'd tried to keep a blue tongue lizard in a tank. He'd loved that damn lizard and he'd gone to great lengths to catch the right beetles and insects to feed it, but he'd been forced to release it when it showed obvious signs of distress.

How could he expect to share his life with a northern hemisphere girl like Charity? His own mother had grabbed the very first chance to hurry back to Scotland and she'd never returned.

On the third morning he stepped on to the back veranda and almost straight away he sensed a difference in Lavender, Annie's Border collie. Her ears were pricked, her tail wagging, and she was quivering with excitement. When she saw Kane she started a frenzied scamper up and down the veranda.

'Well, I'll be...'

'For heaven's sake, look at Lavender,' Charity said when she came out. She was on her way to the laundry with a basket of linen that didn't really need washing. She set the basket down and held out her arms to Lavender and was almost bowled backwards by a leaping black and white torpedo of doggy ecstasy.

'Steady on, girl. What have you been taking?' She laughed as she gently held the dog at bay.

'Annie must be coming home,' Kane said. It was the only explanation. 'Somehow Lavender always knows when Annie's on her way. She's probably hitched a ride with the mailman.' The mail truck did a twice weekly loop from Mirrabrook, past all the stations in Star Valley, and back to town again.

Charity paused in the motion of scooping up the washing basket. 'The mailman?' she repeated. 'Does he double as a taxi driver?'

Kane nodded. 'He doesn't make a habit of it, but lots of locals have been known to cadge a lift with—'

She was looking at him so strangely that he didn't finish the sentence.

'Would the mailman give *me* a lift into Mirrabrook?' she asked.

Kane felt as if he'd swallowed rocks. He tried to clear his throat. 'Sure,' he said. 'If you're in a hurry to get away.'

'Well, if Annie's going to be here, I should go. You won't need me then. Tim's involvement in the trial is over and I'd like to go to Townsville to do a spot of sightseeing with him. I could try to see the Great Barrier Reef.'

'Yes, of course. Good idea.' Kane hooked his thumbs through the belt loops in his jeans and stared at the floorboards, trying to look a hell of a lot more casual and less desolate than he felt.

So this was it; she was going.

'As soon as I've put these things in the washing machine, I'll start packing,' she said.

He risked a glance in her direction and saw that her shoulders were back, as if she were bracing herself against a high wind. She looked pale.

And breathtakingly vulnerable.

Her big green eyes were sad, yet shining with determination. Why? Because she needed to get away? To be free?

'Forget the washing,' he muttered. 'Attend to your packing. The mail truck could be here any time in the next hour.'

'Right,' she said and her eyes shimmered

with a sudden suspicious brightness. 'I wouldn't want to keep the mailman waiting.'

She turned and took a step towards the doorway.

'Chaz.' Kane's throat closed on the word and he half-expected that she hadn't heard him.

But she whirled around sharply. 'Yes?'

'I just wanted to say—' He swallowed. 'Sometimes it's hard to say goodbye properly when there are others around.'

'Yes,' she whispered.

'In case I don't get to say so later—I wanted to let you know—'

Two spots of colour appeared in her cheeks and he lost the thread of what he'd been planning to say.

'Ahh—' He cleared his throat. 'Don't forget—when you start hunting for a husband back in England—you've got to aim high. You deserve someone from the top shelf.'

'Thank you.' The bright glitter in her eyes flashed in the morning sunlight. 'If I ever decide to hunt for a husband, I'll try to remember your advice.'

'And thanks for filling in here. You've fitted in amazingly well.'

'Not bad for an English chick?'

He could see that she was trying unsuccessfully to smile and he almost groaned. 'Not bad at all. You've been—fantastic.'

Her neat teeth showed as she bit her lip. Then she turned away quickly and he found himself staring at her slim white neck. Her hair was twisted up into a casual knot, leaving her neck bare and unprotected. So white. Such a contrast to the bright brandy colour of her hair.

'One other thing,' he said.

She stiffened, but didn't turn back to him.

'You're the most beautiful woman I've ever seen.'

'Oh.'

She was trembling. As he watched, she closed her eyes and seemed to sway on her feet.

Pierced by a swift, burning dismay, he closed the gap between them. As he hauled her into his arms, he felt her tremors vibrate in unison with his own.

'Oh, God, Chaz, I've got to kiss you.'

'Please,' she whispered, tilting her head and offering her lovely warm lips to him.

His breath caught. Need pounded through him. Never had lips been so softly pink and perfect.

Forcing himself to be gentle, he trailed supersensitive fingertips down her smooth white arms till he reached her elbows. Then her waist. And he thought his heart might shoot right out of his chest as he touched his mouth to hers.

Never had a woman been sweeter or more inviting. Her kiss was the loveliest thing he'd ever known. He wanted to lose himself in her like a wild bee plunging the depths of sweet honeysuckle.

And the wonder of it was that she seemed to be driven by the same incomprehensible longing. She pressed her slender curves into him and circled his neck with her arms and her mouth was warm and willing and generous.

With surprising speed their kiss turned hungry, and his hands were in her hair, plundering the rich, silky splendour of it. He kissed her face and the delicate hollow at the base of her neck where a pulse beat wildly beneath her translucent skin.

A soft groan broke from him and he drew her hard against him and, to his amazement, she wasn't put off by the blatant evidence of his desire. She moved against him, twisting and pressing without restraint, kissing him harder, deeper.

In a blinding flash of clarity he realised that their bodies were shouting loudly and honestly what neither of them had dared to whisper. But oh, God, was this wise?

The problem was, right now the only wisdom he could recognise involved taking this woman.

Perhaps there was still time...

Then again, perhaps not...

A few feet from them, Lavender burst into a frenzy of barking. Kane tried to ignore the dog... He gathered Charity even closer, not wanting to break the kiss. Not ever. But, damn it, Lavender's barking probably meant she'd heard the truck coming.

Sure enough, seconds later the sound of a motor reached him. Reluctantly, he pulled away and turned to see a blur of black and white as Lavender scampered down the steps and across the grass and disappeared around the side of the house.

Shaken and a little out of breath, he dropped his forehead to rest against Charity's. With his eyes closed, he felt the slenderness of her waist beneath his hands, felt the silky warmth of her hair against his cheek, smelt the freshness of her shirt and the womanly scent of her skin and he had to bite down hard on a moan of frustration. If only...

There were just too many if onlys... If only he hadn't waited so long. There was no time now to work out what this kiss really meant. If only he hadn't made such a fuss about those crazy house rules.

If only he could keep her.

If only she wanted to stay.

From the front of the homestead came the strident sound of a horn.

'That sounds like the mail truck,' she said.

He didn't answer.

And then... 'Hey, Kane, where are you?' came a cry from the front of the house.

He stole one more possessively urgent kiss from her, then called, 'Coming, Annie.'

He wanted to tell Charity to forget the packing. But she was already turning away from him. If she'd looked up he might have pleaded with her, but she kept walking away and he remembered her air of determination when she had said she wanted to leave...

As she stumbled to her room, Charity's vision was so blurred she could hardly see. She dragged her suitcase from beneath her bed, opened drawers and scooped up garments, but she was shaking so badly the clothes spilled from her arms and fell any which way into the case.

Kane's kiss had turned her inside out.

Inside out, upside down and back to front.

In those few short moments, he'd stirred her body unbearably and stolen her heart completely.

And now she was expected to pack.

Tears slid down her face as she shoved underwear and T-shirts, shoes and dresses into the suitcase with little thought for order. How could she possibly do anything in an orderly fashion when her thoughts and emotions were in such chaos?

Did Kane have any idea what a kiss like that could do to a girl? Especially an inexperienced romantic like her. No doubt he thought nothing of it. He and Marsha probably exchanged kisses like that on a regular basis— along with all manner of intimacies.

O-o-oh. In anger she dumped her boots on top of a silk blouse. It was stupid to think about Kane. And just as stupid to read too much significance into that kiss. She couldn't use her own limited experience as a yardstick. Until now she'd only ever found romance to be mildly pleasant at best, but that didn't mean that other people didn't share wonderful, soul-shattering, passionate kisses on a daily basis.

In Kane's arms, she'd had a taste of the real thing. She'd felt as if fire had been injected under her skin...as if she'd been given wings... And she'd been overcome by such a terrible longing that she now feared it would haunt her for ever.

How could she bear it?

Why had she been so eager to leave Southern Cross?

Was it too impossible to dash outside and tell Kane she'd changed her mind and that she'd like to stay? Would he be shocked?

From the kitchen she could hear excited chatter. A young woman, who must be Annie, seemed to be talking ten to the dozen. Every so often Ted the mailman's chuckle punctuated the conversation. But, although his laughter sounded jovial, Charity knew that he'd interrupted his morning's schedule to do her a favour.

She had no idea if she was welcome to stay on at Southern Cross now that Annie was home. And Reid was about to return with this legendary cook he'd found. What excuse could she give the McKinnons? *I've developed a monumental crush on Kane?*

Feeling wretched, she hurried to the bathroom to fetch her toothbrush and shampoo. What else did she need to collect? She couldn't think. Back in her bedroom, her mind spun miserably as she zipped her toiletry bag.

When a knock sounded on the bedroom door behind her, she jumped.

She whirled around to find a slim blonde woman with twinkling eyes and a warm smile standing in the doorway. Close behind her was Lavender, her tail wagging blissfully.

'Sorry,' the woman said. 'I didn't mean to startle you.'

'I'm afraid my mind was miles away. You must be Annie.'

'Yes.' Annie smiled and extended her hand. 'Pleased to meet you, Charity.'

Annie's hair was fairer than Kane's, but her eyes were the same silvery-blue and her body, while feminine and slim, had the same toned athletic grace. As they shook hands Annie said, 'I'm sorry this is hello and goodbye. Kane said you're keen to head off into town with Ted.'

Actually, no.

If only she knew Annie well enough to confide in her. If only she knew whether Kane had felt what she had when they'd kissed...

'I'm planning to meet up with my brother in Townsville.'

Annie nodded. 'It's great news about the trial, isn't it?'

'Yes.'

'I'm glad Tim's got that behind him. Now he can get on with enjoying himself.'

'That's right.'

Annie folded her arms across her chest and leant her hip against the doorjamb with an easy confidence that Charity couldn't help admiring. 'I hear you've saved Kane from starvation while I've been away.'

Charity shrugged, not sure she could offer even the most casual comment about Kane without giving her feelings away. 'Your brothers insisted that I borrow some of your clothes,' she said. 'I'm afraid I've been wearing your hat and boots and quite a few of your shirts.'

'No worries. You're welcome.'

'Thanks. I've put them all back in your room.'

Annie nodded. 'How are you going with your packing? Can I give you a hand?' Her bright eyes darted around the room as if she was checking for anything left behind.

Following her gaze, Charity shook her head. 'I think I have everything.'

'Great. I don't want to rush you, but I think Ted's eager to get on his way.'

'Yes, of course.'

Charity zipped her suitcase and lifted it on to the floor.

'Kane can carry that for you.' Before Charity could protest, Annie called, 'Kane! Make yourself useful and bring your muscles in here where they're needed.'

Charity's heart began to pound when she heard the sound of his riding boots coming along the hallway to her room. She made a business of checking the contents of her hand-bag—purse, passport, compact, keys for her suitcase, comb, and her souvenir of Southern Cross—a smooth river-washed stone with a fossilised fern embedded in it.

She didn't look up when Kane came into the room.

'Anything else?' he asked, lifting her suit-case.

She pretended to be searching for some-thing in the bottom of her handbag and shook her head without looking up. 'No, just the one case.'

'Right.'

She was tremulously aware of his presence in the room and of her desperate feelings of longing. She couldn't, mustn't, look at him. If her eyes connected with his, she might break down.

'All set?' asked Annie cheerily.

'Yes.'

Annie turned and walked back down the hall.

With a gentlemanly sweep of his hand, Kane indicated that Charity should follow.

She dipped her head in his direction and walked out of the room, and he followed her down the hallway, through the house to the front veranda.

Ted, a wizened, brown-faced man, was waiting beside the mail truck. He sent her a curt nod of greeting.

'I'm sorry I didn't get a chance to get to know you, Charity,' Annie said. 'I would have appreciated some female company. Now I'm going to be surrounded by blokes again. But you never know, I might see you soon. I'm thinking of coming to the UK to visit my mother.'

'Then you must certainly come to Hollydean,' Charity told her. Out of the corner of her eye she watched Kane heft her suitcase into the back of the truck. 'You'd be very welcome to stay with us. We have plenty of room.'

'Thanks, I'll remember that.'

Annie's enthusiasm seemed to dominate the farewells. By the time Kane returned from loading the suitcase, Ted had opened the driver's door and was obviously itching to get on the road.

Annie accompanied Charity around to the passenger door. Leaning forward, she gave Charity a quick kiss on the cheek. 'Say hello to Tim for me and have a safe journey.'

'Thanks, I will.'

Kane appeared behind Annie. 'Goodbye, Chaz,' he said.

'Goodbye.' Her mouth formed the words but no sound came out.

'All set, then?' called Ted from the other side of the truck.

When Kane stepped forward his kiss on her cheek was just as light and quick as Annie's had been. Nevertheless, Charity's skin tingled where his lips touched her and flames shot up her spine when he placed his hand at the small of her back as she stepped up into the truck.

Safely inside, she lifted her eyes and looked at him through the truck's dusty window. Oh, God. One look at his frozen, pain-filled face and she wanted to haul the door open, to leap down into his arms. She wanted to cling to him and beg him to let her stay.

But already the truck was pulling away. And Kane was lifting his hand to send her one swift, stiff wave.

When the truck was halfway to the front

gate she squirmed in her seat and saw that Annie was laughing as she threw an arm around her brother's shoulders. And, as the scrub closed in around the track, she caught one last glimpse of Annie pulling back and staring at Kane with a very worried frown on her face.

CHAPTER TEN

'I'M SORRY, Charity. I've already made other plans.' Tim's eyes were luminous with apology.

He'd taken her to a café on the Townsville Strand, where they could look clear across the shimmering waters of Cleveland Bay to green, hilly Magnetic Island. She'd been enchanted by her first sight of this view, but now Tim's news robbed the whole scene of its lustre.

'I really am very sorry,' he said. 'If I'd any idea that you wanted to do some sightseeing while you were here, I would never have signed up, but I've made a firm commitment now and the yacht leaves for New Zealand the day after tomorrow. The skipper wants to get well south of here before the cyclone season starts.'

Ice clinked loudly in Charity's glass as she stirred her lemon lime and bitters with angry strikes of her straw. 'Do you think you should be heading off across the ocean when you don't know the first thing about sailing?'

Tim scowled and tension tightened his jaw. A muscle jerked in his cheek as he switched his gaze to the distant horizon. She followed his gaze. Somewhere out there lay the Great Barrier Reef with its beautiful coral and tropical fish, but now she would probably never see it.

'I really want to do this,' he said. 'I've already spoken to Dad and there's a satellite phone on the yacht, so I'll be able to keep in touch.'

She sighed and tried to shake off her disappointment. It stung that her brother hadn't given her a thought when he'd made his plans, but she knew that at nineteen most young people went through degrees of selfishness. Tim was making his place in the world, but ever since she'd left Southern Cross she'd felt as if her own world was falling apart.

'I guess it's high time I stopped asking snoopy big sister questions,' she said. 'I'm sure you'll adapt to sailing as quickly as you did to mustering cattle and you'll have a wonderful adventure.'

'But you should have an adventure too. You should try to see more of Australia even though I won't be here. If you don't want to go alone you could hook up with some of the

British backpackers that are passing through here every day.'

She smiled but was glad she was wearing sunglasses so he couldn't see that the smile didn't reach her eyes. Taking off on an adventure with a group of strangers required youthful enthusiasm and a carefree heart. Right now, she felt sadly lacking in both.

In the Townsville mall, she found a friendly travel agent and enquired if it was possible to change the booking for her return flight home. She knew it was unlikely that the travel agency could accommodate her at short notice, but it was worth a gamble.

While the smiling fellow in the loud tropical shirt concentrated on his computer screen she glanced outside at the startling Townsville sunshine. There was a garden in the centre of the mall and a frangipani tree with shiny green leaves and lovely flowers with smooth, perfectly white petals and yellow throats.

The tree made her think of Southern Cross. There'd been a frangipani tree in the garden there. She'd floated its beautiful flowers in a flat, circular vase and set them on the sideboard, and their subtle, tropical fragrance had filtered throughout the house.

Thinking about Southern Cross, she let her mind play with the fantasy of going back, and she tried to picture the surprised expressions on the McKinnons' faces if she turned up at their front door.

'You little beauty!' The travel agent's cry brought her back with a start. He sent her a broad, beaming smile. 'You're in luck! I can get you from here to Cairns this afternoon for a link with a flight that will take you straight through to London. You'll be landing at Heathrow inside twenty-four hours. Talk about lucky!'

Shocked, she stared at him.

England.

Tomorrow.

Her gaze shot back out to the sunny mall. In England it would be the end of autumn. There would be leafless trees and pale, wind-swept skies.

Seconds ago, she'd been picturing herself bravely returning to Mirrabrook, seeing Kane again and finding the courage to talk to him honestly…about…about *everything*.

Was fate conspiring against her? It certainly seemed that way. First there'd been the mail truck, then Tim's new burst of independence and now this amazing fluke with the airlines!

It felt for all the world as if the universe was sending her a message. Telling her to forget about Kane McKinnon, to go home…

And, deep down, she suspected that it was pointless to fight it.

'Lucky?' she said, blinking madly. 'Oh, absolutely. That's me. Lucky's my middle name.'

Annie cornered Kane in the tack room where he was cleaning saddles.

'I was hoping I'd find you alone in here, big brother. I'd like to have a sisterly chat.'

He smiled. 'I've been expecting this.' Kneading polish into the leather on a saddle flap, he said, 'I've been waiting for you to tell me what your dash to Brisbane was all about.'

'That's not what I want to talk about now.'

Kane looked up to see a flash of colour come and go in her cheeks.

'Don't worry about me,' she said. 'I've got my own life in hand. It's yours I'm worried about.'

'Mine?' He frowned and reached for more oil. 'What's there to worry about? I'm right as rain.'

Annie shook her head and made a performance of rolling her eyes. 'If you really expect me to believe that, you're dumber than I ever imagined.' After a pause, she leaned closer. 'Anyhow, I'm not just concerned about you, my darling brother. I'm thinking of Charity Denham, too.'

His head jerked up. 'What about her?'

Throwing her hands into the air in a gesture of exasperation, Annie turned and walked away from him, and Kane rubbed at a dull spot on the leather as if his life depended on it. His sister began to circle him slowly and, when he risked a glance in her direction, her face seemed to have grown strangely older, sadder and wiser.

Her eyes sought his. 'If you're going to pretend you don't know what I'm talking about, I could be wasting my time.'

'I'm damn sure you're wasting your time.'

She sighed. 'Let me just say that I did learn one or two things when I was in Brisbane.'

'Yeah?'

'And if you've let Charity go back to England without telling her how you honestly feel—'

To Kane's astonishment, her face crumpled.

'You've committed a terrible crime,' she said and then turned and dashed out of the room.

Throwing his head back, Kane drew a deep breath of summer air and stared out through the doorway to the evening star, already shining brightly in the deep teal sky. And as Annie's words sank home, a dead weight seemed to roll from his shoulders.

But he felt no relief from the bittersweet arrow that pierced his heart.

CHAPTER ELEVEN

'GABRIEL, this is your cue.'

Charity looked towards the doorway where a heavenly host of six-year-old angels was supposed to appear.

'Where's Gabriel?' she called.

The boy standing closest to her, who'd become painfully smug since she'd asked him to play the role of Joseph, shrugged and pulled a don't ask me face.

Raising her hand, she signalled to the organist to hold the introduction to the next carol and she beckoned to one of the shepherds gathered around a flock of toy sheep at the bottom of the chancel steps.

'Simon, can you go and tell the angels they've missed their cue?'

As the eight-year-old dashed off, she ran a distracted hand through her hair. Why on earth had she let herself in for this again? Last year she'd sworn never to direct another Christmas nativity play. And yet here she was putting herself through the same annual torture.

The plays always went well on the day, with parents and parishioners *ooh-ing* and *aah-ing* over the sweet children, but the rehearsals were exhausting.

And this year she had more than the nativity play to test her patience. Sleepless nights were an added problem. And so was her father's gentle insistence that she 'get out and have some fun'. Now that he was so very happy with Alice he wanted to be surrounded by happiness, but for Charity nothing felt like fun any more.

She had never thought that coming home would be so hard.

This was Hollydean, the centre of her life. She had always thought that coming home would be like returning to a beloved sanctuary. But since she'd returned from Southern Cross the sights and places that used to charm and cheer her seemed overly quaint and unnecessarily neat and orderly. The familiar predictability of every cottage, shop-front, field and lane annoyed her.

'The angels are fighting,' Simon the shepherd informed her when he returned.

'Isn't Mrs Waterford there to settle them?'

'No, she's busy outside chatting to some chap.'

'Oh, for goodness' sake.' Charity sent a de-

spairing glance over her assembled cast. 'No
one move till I sort out the angels,' she ordered them. 'Wise men, I'm expecting you to
be ready and waiting at the back of the hall.
Your procession will start as soon as the angels have finished singing. Mary, please don't
undress the baby now.'

As she hurried down the passage to the vestry the sounds of raised voices and sobbing
reached her. 'What on earth's going on out
here?' she cried as she stepped into the vestry.

'Billy broke Dinah's wings,' piped up a
voice.

'Because Dinah bossed him and told him to
stop picking his nose,' added another.

'And now his nose is bleeding.'

'Oh, Billy.' Charity rushed forward. Bright
blood was dripping from the small boy's
freckled nose on to the white sheeting of his
angel costume. He was terrified by the sight
of it, and the moment he saw Charity he began
to wail loudly.

'There, there, you'll be all right,' she
soothed, grabbing a tissue from her pocket.
'Let me tip your head forward a little. That's
right. Good boy.'

Over Billy's head, she spoke to another angel. 'Can you run outside and tell Mrs
Waterford what's happened? Tell her I really

need her in here. Maisie, bring me the box of tissues from the table, please.'

It took the application of several tissues before the bleeding slowed. Gently, Charity pinched the soft part of Billy's nostrils together. 'Breathe through your mouth, Billy,' she instructed.

Silent now, the wide-eyed children crowded close, looking touchingly angelic in their white sheets and wings of cardboard covered with fluffy cotton wool and golden stars. In their midst, Charity, in her green winter dress with her bright hair tied back by an old tartan ribbon, knelt beside Billy.

The vestry door opened and an icy blast swept in from outside as Eileen Waterford rushed into the room.

'I'm so sorry, Charity,' she cried when she saw Billy. 'I just stepped outside for a moment to explain to this gentleman when you would be free and—' She stopped when she saw Charity's face. 'My dear, what's the matter?'

Shock was jolting through Charity like a lightning strike. She felt her blood rush to her toes as she stared at the man who'd walked in behind Eileen.

Kane. What was he doing here?

Flecks of snow gleamed in his hair and on

the dark, wide-shouldered cape of his outback riding coat. His hands were plunged deep into his coat pockets and he was staring down at her with a complicated expression that bewildered her. Was it concern? Amusement?

Eileen shot a worried glance from one to the other. 'You *do* know Mr McKinnon, don't you, Charity?'

'Y-yes,' she whispered, and then she nodded because she knew no one could have heard her reply. Her heart was thudding so violently she hadn't even heard it herself. Oh, God. Her eyes were filling with tears.

Behind her, another crowd of children with striped sheets on their heads appeared in a doorway. The shepherds had grown restless.

'Can you hurry up? We're tired of waiting,' one of them complained.

Heart racing, head swirling, Charity blinked and looked at her watch. She was running out of time. The children's parents would be coming back to collect them in another twenty minutes.

Everyone stared expectantly in her direction, and Kane's voice broke into the room. 'I don't want to interrupt you,' he said. 'I'm happy to wait outside until you're finished.'

The children switched their attention to him, and their eyes grew round with curiosity.

Everything about Kane signalled *difference*—
his outback suntan, the distinctive styling of
his oilskin coat, his Australian accent.

'You can't wait outside in the snow,'
Charity told him tightly. 'It's too cold.'

'Why don't you go in and wait in the
church, Mr McKinnon?' recommended
Eileen. 'It's nice and warm in there.'

Thanks a million, Eileen. Charity bit back
an exclamation of panic. How on earth could
she pull this rehearsal together with Kane
watching her?

Why was he here? What was he thinking?

A faintly bemused smile played over his
features, and yet his eyes reflected an uncer-
tainty that was so uncharacteristic of him that
her poor heart plunged.

Taking a deep breath, she spoke without
looking at Kane again. 'Okay, shepherds, you
go back into the church and take Mr
McKinnon with you. Billy, don't worry, we'll
have your costume clean again before Sunday.
Angels, I want you lined up and ready to come
on straight away. Gabriel, you're the leader.
You know your cue, don't you?'

The boy who was Gabriel nodded.

Everyone returned to their allotted places
and the rehearsal continued.

And somehow Charity got through it.

Kane settled into a pew towards the back of the church and, although it was impossible to forget he was there, she tried valiantly to ignore him. But of course she stole many quick glances his way. He sat very still, with one arm extended along the polished back of the pew and each time her eyes scooted in his direction she found him watching her with a strangely serious smile.

And each time she saw that smile a harrowing thrill darted through her. *Why had he come?*

By the time the children reached the last verse of the last carol, the back of the church was beginning to fill with proud, moist-eyed parents. After that, there was a flurry of activity as children were bundled into warm coats, while Charity gave them last-minute reminders, or chatted with parents, especially Billy's mother, who needed an explanation about his nose.

Kane waited through it all, sitting patiently at the back of the church.

Eventually, the last family left and Charity's stomach was a mass of butterflies as she walked down the aisle towards him. Shaking her head, she tried to laugh. 'Thank heavens that's over.'

He jumped to his feet before she reached

the end of his pew. 'It was terrific,' he said, coming towards her. '*You* were terrific.'

'Thanks.' She felt her cheeks grow hot.

He didn't come any closer. He seemed terribly nervous. There was no greeting kiss.

'This is such a surprise—' she said. 'But it's good to see you, of course.' She drew a deep breath. 'What brings you to England?'

'Annie. She wanted to come to Scotland to visit Mum and I decided to accompany her.'

'I see.' She tried not to sound disappointed. Of course Kane hadn't crossed hemispheres simply to find *her*. 'How is your mother?'

'Very well, thank you.'

'And Annie? Has she come to Hollydean with you?'

'No, she's still in Scotland.'

She let out a little huff of breath, trying to lessen the awful tension inside her. 'So Reid's holding the fort at Southern Cross?'

'Ferret's moved in to give him an extra hand.'

'And—' Oh, dear, how long could she keep this up? 'How is the little premature baby?'

'She's growing faster than grass in the wet season.'

'That's wonderful.'

Too soon she'd exhausted her questions about other people. Which left *them*... 'I don't suppose you were expecting to sit through a nativity play.'

'I didn't mind at all,' he said. 'It was very educational.'

'Educational?' She risked a tiny, curious smile. 'Aren't you familiar with the Christmas story?'

His answering smile was heartbreakingly nervous. 'I know it well. What I meant was I learned a lot more about you.'

'Oh.' She glanced down at her hands and interlaced her fingers, then released them again.

'I've been forced to see you in a different light.'

'As a Sunday school teacher?'

'Yes,' he said slowly.

Looking up, she watched his gaze travel over the interior of the church—taking in the stained glass windows, the paintings of the apostles hanging on the stone walls, the high, vaulted ceiling and the altar with its gleaming candlesticks and cross. Then back to her.

'Are you ready to leave yet?' he asked.

'Yes, of course. My coat's in the vestry.'

She had never felt more self-conscious walking down the aisle of St Alban's than she did now as she walked beside Kane. She found herself remembering hundreds of girlish daydreams in which she'd pictured herself walking down this very aisle with a wonderful man at her side. She'd never been able to see the exact face of that man, but oh, how fiercely she had loved him.

For years she'd been in love with him. He was tall and handsome and tender and always, *always,* passionately, desperately in love with her.

Could he be Kane McKinnon?

She wanted it to be him. She wanted it so badly she was trembling.

In the vestry, he helped her with her coat and scarf and her skin flashed heat as his fingers brushed lightly against the back of her neck.

'How are you finding our weather?' she managed to ask, tucking her crimson scarf inside her coat as the freezing air nipped them when they stepped outside. 'Do you mind the wind and the snow?'

'The weather's great,' he said. 'The snow's beautiful. I'm loving every flake. It's so different from home.'

'It's unusual for us to have snow so early. It actually looks like we might have a white Christmas this year.'

As they walked side by side down the stone

path beside the church she saw that he'd thrust his hands back into his pockets.

'You need gloves,' she said, holding up her hands to show him her lovely fur-lined crimson leather gloves that had been last year's Christmas present from her father.

'I sure do.' He grinned. 'It's my turn to be out of my environment now.'

She tried to imagine how this scene must look through Kane's eyes—the snowy churchyard, the winter-bare trees and the ancient gravestones with mottled green lichen showing beneath lacy veils of snow.

'This part of the world is the exact opposite of yours,' she said.

'Yeah. It's kind of scary.'

'Scary? At least we don't have red bellied black snakes. I can't believe tough Kane McKinnon is scared of a little snow?'

'Well—it's not the snow exactly—it's—it's *everything*—' Throwing his head back, he stared up at the pale frosty sky and dragged in a ragged breath. 'It makes me realise—'

He looked at her again and his blue eyes were anxious. Dear heaven, was this really the same confident, cocky fellow who'd taken such delight in teasing her when she'd first arrived in the outback?

His mouth quirked into another strangely sad smile. 'Annie was just an excuse, Chaz.'

She came to an abrupt halt and stared at him, hardly daring to breathe.

'I came here to see you,' he said. 'I've been driving myself crazy ever since you left.

'I thought about telephoning you,' he said. 'Or writing to you, but I was worried I'd stuff it up. I needed to *see* you. But now that I'm here, I realise I was mad to think—' He broke off and looked away, his face tightening.

A muscle beneath his cheekbone twitched and the corners of his mouth pulled down, as if he were battling with a deep emotion. 'You're an English rose, Chaz. This is where you belong. We don't even have a regular minister in the Star Valley—just a bush padre who comes through once a month to conduct a service in Mirrabrook.'

He looked so distressed her heart nearly broke for him. He had no idea how hopelessly in love she was. In love with *him*. Falling in love wasn't about choosing a place to live. It was this man who mattered. It was this man she wanted.

'Kane, ever since I came home I haven't been able to stop thinking about you.'

His blue eyes burned against the bleak mid-winter backdrop. 'Really?'

'Not for a minute.'

He took a step towards her.

Her heart tumbled. 'I have the worst possible crush on you, Kane McKinnon.' She reached out and touched his sleeve lightly. 'I'd appreciate it very much if you could put me out of my misery.'

He seemed unable to speak as he stared at her gloved hand resting on his forearm.

Whispering, she asked, 'Could you possibly kiss me without taking your hands out of your pockets?'

His face broke into a gorgeous smile, like sunshine bursting through clouds. 'That's an incredibly sexy question, Sunday school teacher.'

'So what's your answer, cattleman?' Never in her life had she asked a man to kiss her.

His smile lingered. And, with his hands in his pockets, he dipped his head till his lips found hers. 'I'll give it my best shot,' he murmured against her mouth.

Softly, slowly, he kissed her.

And his kiss was even more wonderful than she remembered. Gentle at first, he teased her lips with his, then gradually he nipped and tasted her mouth, coaxing her to relax and to absorb every delightful sensation. She had to cling to the lapels of his coat for balance, but she gloried in the way he took his sweet time with her.

It was so amazing, and she knew, just *knew*, that this was exactly how her life was meant to be. Right now. Right here. With Kane. Sharing kisses like this. And this. And *this*.

Without lifting his lips from hers or taking his hands from his pockets, Kane shepherded her backwards till her hips came to rest against a stone buttress. And, with the support at her back, their kiss took on a whole new level of excitement.

Now she could pull him close, hard against her, where she needed him. The only problem was the bulk of their coats, which denied her the contact she craved. She wanted to feel Kane's skin. She could picture the sleek bronzed wonder of it as it stretched like satin over his muscles.

Their bodies strained together, fighting the barrier of their coats. Kane pressed into her and his tongue drove deep and her body burned and trembled with the overwhelming thrill of it.

Then suddenly, when she thought the surrounding snow might melt from the heat of her desire, Kane lifted his head.

'What the blazes was I thinking?' he muttered against her ear. 'I've got you up against the church wall.'

'It doesn't matter,' she whispered. 'I might be a clergyman's daughter, but I'm no saint.'

He laughed and she laughed too, feeling breathless as she lifted away from the wall and dropped her head to rest against his chest.

Too late, she realised that Kane's hands were still wedged in his pockets and that the movement had shifted their point of balance. Before either of them could adjust, they were toppling sideways into the soft, freshly fallen snow.

As they fell, Charity grabbed at Kane's coat and brought him down on top of her. But her startled cry was silenced as his mouth found hers once more.

Oh, my. Oh, wow! How sensational. Kane's full length covered her now. How deliciously abandoned and wicked it was to lie in the snow with him and to give in to all kinds of seductive impulses. She heard his low chuckle.

'Have you ever been kissed in the snow, Chaz?'

'Not while I was horizontal. Have you?'

'Can't say I have.'

His lips were surprisingly warm and so

were his hands which, free of his pockets now, cradled her face, dived through her hair…

Her body grew hot and tight.

She was a sexy snow siren…

Until…

He lifted his head. 'What if someone sees us?'

She glanced over his shoulder towards the rectory. 'Oh dear, I think they already have.'

He turned to look where she was looking—at her father and Alice, standing together at the big window in the dining room, staring straight at them with their mouths gaping.

Kane groaned. 'Is that who I think it is?'

'My father? 'Fraid so.'

Letting out a cry of dismay, he thrust his bare hands into the snow and pushed himself away from her and, with an agility that shouldn't have surprised her, he sprang to his feet.

'Chaz, I'm sorry.' He helped her up and dusted snow from her coat and hair. 'The last thing I wanted was to embarrass you.'

She smiled. 'Don't worry. Father's so hopelessly in love at the moment he won't mind a bit.' She slipped her arm through his. 'At least he won't mind once he's met you and discovers how wonderful you are.'

She heard Kane inhale sharply. But he

didn't look so nervous any more and another glance towards the rectory showed that her father and Alice had retreated.

'Anyway, I'm not going to bother you with introductions just yet,' she said. 'For now, my father can wait.'

'Are you sure?'

'Absolutely.' Grabbing Kane's hands, she rubbed at them. 'Let's get you in out of the cold.' She began to pull him along the path, away from the church.

'Where are we going?'

'My place.' Her heart skipped several beats as she said that.

'But I thought you lived over there,' he said, nodding his head in the direction of the rectory.

'Not any more.' She smiled at his bewilderment. 'When father and Alice were married, I moved into my own cottage down the lane. Actually, it's Alice's cottage. We swapped homes. It's an arrangement that's suited us both very well—at least for the time being.'

He looked surprised but absurdly pleased.

'Come and see. It's a lovely cottage and it's very close by.' Leaving the churchyard, they headed down narrow Holly Lane and within a few minutes, rounded a corner. 'There it is,' she said, pointing. 'The cottage with the green door.'

Alice's place was very old, but it was wonderfully picturesque—one and a half storeys, with windows and doors at all sorts of odd angles—all peeping comfortably from beneath a blanket of snow.

'It's quite charming, isn't it?'

He nodded. 'Very. Like something you'd see on a Christmas card.'

'And it's super cosy,' she added. 'There's a warm fire, warm bed.'

Kane stopped dead in his tracks and she almost lost her balance again. Gripping her elbows, he turned her to face him and his eyes searched her face. Her stomach flipped as if she'd been shot into outer space.

'Bed?' he whispered. 'Are you sure about this?'

She looked steadfastly into his eyes—the beautiful silver-blue eyes that she loved—and she knew that she'd spent far too long suppressing her feelings for this man.

'Yes, Kane, I'm very sure.' She had never been more certain of anything.

His fingers reached to touch a strand of her hair that curled like a copper coil against the black collar of her coat. 'Charity, you know that if I come to the cottage with you now,' he said, 'there will be no turning back.'

She smiled. 'That's what I'm banking on.'

CHAPTER TWELVE

PERHAPS he was dreaming.

How had this happened so quickly? A short time ago he'd been sitting at the back of St Alban's church, convinced that he'd made a terrible mistake...that he shouldn't have come...that it would be totally wrong to tell Charity Denham how he felt about her.

He'd watched her with those children and he'd seen how they adored her—even the little monsters he'd wanted to thump—and he'd been stricken with terrible doubts. This was Charity's *life*. Hollydean was where she belonged.

He had no right to arrive unannounced from the outback with hopes that would turn her world upside-down.

And yet...

It seemed, by some miracle, that he was exactly what Charity wanted. And she wanted him *now*. The kiss in the churchyard had shot his doubts to pieces.

Fresh snow began to fall softly as they walked up the path to her front door.

Charity jiggled the key in the lock. 'I'm afraid this lock is dodgy,' she said. 'I have to get the key at exactly the right angle.'

'Would you like me to try?'

She wiggled it from left to right and back again. 'No, it's okay. I've got it.' Then she gave the door a shove with her shoulder and it swung open to reveal a front parlour. 'You might have to duck your head; the lintel's a bit low.' She shot him a shy smile over her shoulder. 'And perhaps you should keep your coat on for a bit, until the fire's warmed the place up.'

He waited in the middle of the room as she pulled off her gloves and began to dart about, turning on lamps, lighting the fire and switching on the flashing lights on the little Christmas tree in the corner. Watching her, he wondered if she was nervous and he felt his heart pound in time with the tree lights.

Red. Blue. Green. Gold.

'Can I get you a drink?' she asked. 'Something warm, perhaps?'

'I'm fine, thank you.'

A moment later, he thought that he perhaps he should have accepted a drink. It would have given them time to adjust to this new situation. He looked around the cottage and saw the clutter of art equipment scattered on the dining table in the adjoining room, and walked towards it. 'You've started painting?'

'Just a few Christmas cards.'

'May I look?'

She nodded, and he picked up a card and held it carefully between his fingertips. 'Hey, you've painted Australian gum leaves.'

'Yes.'

She'd painted in water colour—a Christmas wreath of eucalypt leaves in a mixture of shades—new, pink-tipped growth, dusty blue-green leaves and faded khaki, adorned with a gauzy, pale gold bow and an arrangement of ragged pink gum blossoms and smooth brown nuts.

'What do you think? Is it okay?' she asked.

'Okay? It's bloody fantastic. I had no idea you were so good, Chaz. This is great. It's beautiful.'

'I wanted to paint Australian things while they were fresh in my mind.'

'You've got them exactly right. I can almost smell the eucalyptus in those gum leaves. I'm no art expert, but I'm sure you're a genius.'

She pulled a face, but seemed pleased. 'I sent a card to Southern Cross. It should be arriving there any day now.' Then she said, 'This room heats up quite quickly. I'll take your coat now if you like.'

'Thanks,' he said, almost absentmindedly, barely shifting his gaze from the other cards on the table as he flipped buttons open and shrugged out of his coat. The other paintings were all variations on the gum leaf theme. All lovely. All brilliant.

When she returned from hanging their coats, she said softly, 'I seem to have developed a *thing* for Australia.'

Muscles in his throat worked as he turned to her.

She looked lovely in the soft light and a kind of helplessness came over him.

'You are incredibly special, Chaz. I wish I had the words to tell you.' Feeling inadequate, he shook his head and rubbed his hand over the back of his neck. 'In the bush, we get out of the habit of expressing ourselves. Some of the blokes I work with probably don't use more than two adjectives or adverbs in a month. I—I should have scoured the dictionary—'

'I don't need words, Kane.'

'But you *deserve* words.' He reached for her hands and held them in his. 'You deserve beautiful words. Delicate words. Stunning words. I should have read poetry. There are wonderful words for what's happening inside me, but I don't seem to be able to let them out.'

'You worry too much.' She dropped her gaze to their linked hands. 'What if I tell you about the poetry that's happening inside me?'

'Okay.' He swallowed. 'Fire away.'

Lifting her eyes, she smiled coyly. 'I have a burning ambition, that comes from the depths of my—um—insides—to see firelight dancing on your bare skin.'

Kane laughed. Tipping his head back, he let the laughter roll and felt some of the tension leave him. 'That's not fair, woman. I'm trying to be earnest and sincere.'

'So am I.'

'You're being sincerely seductive.'

'Yes. Is it working?'

He pulled her close. 'Damn right it is.' He kissed her neck just below her ear.

'Mmm… I'll accept kisses instead of words.'

'Maybe kisses can *be* words,' he whispered back and he scattered tender kisses over her throat and beneath her chin. She made a low, soft sound, a breath-catching gasp and he lifted her bright hair to kiss the back of her lovely pale neck. 'These kisses are saying that

Charity Denham is more beautiful than sunset on snow.'

He kissed her throat, her forehead, her soft cheeks, her delicate eyelids. 'And these are saying how much I love you.'

A happy cry broke from her, but he silenced it with his lips on hers. His arms enfolded her, drawing her slender curves close. He kissed her deeply, ardently. Wanting her to feel and taste his love for her, wanting her to understand that his love sprang from some soul-deep place that belonged to her and only to her.

When at last he released her, she whispered, 'Oh, wow! I think I know what that kiss was saying.'

'That I'm going to love you for ever.'

Her eyes shone as she lifted her hands to frame his face. 'My turn,' she said and she pulled his head down and kissed him back the same way he'd kissed her. 'This kiss is saying that I love you too, Kane McKinnon. My biggest mistake was to leave Southern Cross.'

'Mine was to let you go. Thank heavens I listened to Annie.'

'What did she say?'

'She told me it was criminal to let you go without telling you how much I love you.'

'I knew I liked your sister.'

They kissed again.

And this time when their lips met they both knew that no more words were needed.

Now...bathed in the fire's warmth...with the snow falling soundlessly outside...and with Christmas tree lights flickering through the gathering shadows...it was time for caresses, for tender discovery...for honest embraces... For loving.

CHAPTER THIRTEEN

IN MID-JANUARY, the snow was still lying like a smooth white blanket over the rooftops and streets of Hollydean, but inside the expanded dining room of the Hollydean Arms the atmosphere was warm and bright and filled with the laughter of happy guests.

Charity, her best friend Emma and her stepmother Alice had been busy setting dozens of candles within fairy tale wreaths of ivy, white chrysanthemums and burgundy rosebuds. And now, from the deep stone windowsills and from every table, romantic candlelight sparkled and was reflected in the many windows that flanked three sides of the room.

The assembled guests were mostly members of the congregation of St Alban's, but of course Kane's mother was there, looking very elegant and immensely proud. And Annie had come, looking a little too thin and pale, but rather beautiful in a soft heather-blue wool dress shot with silver thread.

Reid hadn't been able to leave Southern

Cross, but Tim had arrived home in the nick of time, suntanned after his adventure at sea, and looking impossibly grown-up in his formal suit.

Charity beamed radiant smiles at them all as she sat beside Kane in her beautiful, scoop-necked, long-sleeved, ivory velvet wedding gown, which Hollydean's most sought after dressmaker had created in a miraculously short time.

This was it. Her wedding day.

The ceremony performed by her father in St Alban's had unfolded like the most beautiful of her happiest dreams. And now she and her tall, tender, passionate lover had declared their love before God and the world.

Talk about blissed-out! The day was passing in a dizzying, happy blur. It was hard to believe that already the reception was in full swing. Jack Houghton, the local headmaster and her father's oldest friend, was proposing his toast to the bride and groom.

'Kane McKinnon is quite a splendid chap,' Jack was saying. 'And, although I've heard it claimed that it's impossible to love and to be wise, I'd like to suggest that Kane has managed both. I'm sure you'll all agree that a man who chose Charity Denham as his bride has displayed indisputable wisdom.'

There was a huge burst of applause and Charity felt her cheeks heat to match the crushed strawberry velvet of Emma's brides-maid's dress. She waved to her girlfriends, who had formed a spontaneous cheer squad, whistling and cheering as they sent her cheeky thumbs-up signals.

'But this bridegroom has also won Charity's heart,' Jack continued. 'And anyone who knows our dear lass will know that Kane must have demonstrated a deep and abiding love for her. She wouldn't have had it any other way.'

Charity turned to Kane, her eyes shining. Each time she looked at him today her heart seemed to swell to bursting point. Reaching out, she touched her hand to his and he squeezed hers in answer.

Their eyes connected. *Oh, dear heaven. He looks worried.*

What was the matter?

She heard little of the rest of Jack's toast. Dimly, she was aware that the guests were standing with their glasses raised.

'To the bride and groom,' Jack said. 'Let's drink to the health, wealth and happiness of Charity and Kane.'

Around them floated the chorus: 'To

Charity and Kane.' And then there was a thunderous wave of applause.

Charity tried to smile, but she was too concerned for Kane. She'd suddenly realised that he must be nervous about responding to this toast. That had to be the problem. Why hadn't she considered this possibility?

How could she have been so thoughtless? She'd been so busy with the whirlwind preparations that she hadn't given a thought to Kane's speaking commitment. And now this huge crowd of strangers was expecting him to respond to Jack's eloquent toast. Her throat tightened with sympathy.

How could she have overlooked this? Was he prepared? Did he have notes? No doubt he would prefer to face a black snake or a wild scrub bull than speak in front of all these people. But it was too late to rescue him now. Already, he was being called upon to speak. She sent up a swift prayer as he rose to his feet.

Standing beside her, stiff as a soldier, he looked out at the expectant crowd, his expression intense, unsmiling. She could see the slide of his Adam's apple above his starched white collar as he swallowed.

All eyes were on him as he stood there, not speaking.

Any minute now, the lengthy silence would become awkward. Embarrassing. Her heart began to pound.

And then at last Kane spoke. 'Ladies and gentlemen...' He stopped and ran a finger around the inside of his collar.

Charity wanted to tell him not to worry. It didn't matter. Of course it didn't. She hoped that her friends would understand how wonderful he was...just how lucky she was.

She sent him an encouraging smile, and he stared at her for the longest time.

Then he returned her smile slowly... beautifully...squared his shoulders and looked out once more at their guests.

'Ladies and gentlemen, today Charity Fleur Denham, this most beautiful bride since time began, promised to be my wife until we're parted by death.' He paused and drew a deep breath. 'No man has accepted a greater honour.'

All in a rush, her eyes filled with happy tears.

Resting his hand on her shoulder, he grinned. 'And at last I know her middle name.'

Everyone laughed, including Charity, and then Kane went on. 'I want to thank every one of you in this room for the part you've played in today's happiness. First my mother, who raised me and taught me to recognise a good woman when I found one. And Matthew, Charity's father—for—for raising a miracle—and for performing our moving wedding ceremony.

'Neither Charity nor I could let this day go past without paying tribute to her mother, Fleur, or my father, Cob, who are no longer with us, but who hold timeless places in our hearts.'

Smiling through happy tears, Charity reached up and clasped Kane's strong brown hand where it rested on her shoulder.

'I can't neglect my sister, Annie. I owe you one, sis.' There was a pause while brother and sister shared a private smile. 'And we also owe an enormous debt to Charity's brother, Tim. He's done a sterling job today as my best man, but some of you may not know that his sister and I would never have met if he hadn't had a craving for adventure in Australia.'

Tim gave a cheery wave, jumped to his feet and bowed deeply, while everyone laughed indulgently.

'But finally, before I propose a toast to Tim and to Charity's lovely bridesmaid, Emma, I want to thank all of you good folk of Hollydean. Thank you for welcoming me here and for trusting me with a very special woman. I know you love Charity almost as much as I do and I know you're going to miss her. I want to thank you for letting me take her back to the wilds of the outback.

'I promise you won't lose her and I'm determined not to lose the new friends I've made here. Please remember that the welcome mat is always out at Southern Cross. It's different down under, but I'm sure you'll enjoy it and there's plenty of room. We could probably fit the whole of Derbyshire on our property.'

Charity grinned at the happy thought of hosting friends and family at Southern Cross homestead.

'We'll be back,' Kane added. 'And we apologise in advance for the noisy but endearing children we plan to bring with us.'

Laughter floated around the room and Charity rose quickly to give Kane an ecstatic hug. Had there ever been a more gorgeous, sensitive, brilliant bridegroom?

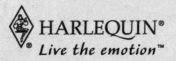

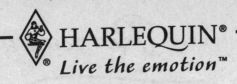

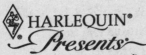

From first love to forever, these love stories
are fairy tale romances for today's woman.

Modern, passionate reads that are powerful and provocative.

Emotional, compelling stories that capture the intensity
of living, loving and creating a family in today's world.

A roller-coaster read that delivers romantic thrills
in a world of suspense, adventure and more.

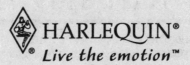